TWO NOVELLA
by
Allan Ishmael Young

THE HEAD ROCK CHALLENGE
and
THE CROSSROADS STORE

TWO NOVELLAS
by Allan Ishmael Young

THE HEAD ROCK CHALLENGE

Lord, how I hate these people, kept running through his mind. Life seems to smite him at every turn. His personal as well as his professional life, are constantly full of insurmountable problems. His inherent dislike of family members and potential friends slowly turns to hate. When eventually he comes to believe that he has found ways to conquer his difficulties, he makes his flight from the area in his own way.

THE CROSSROADS STORE

This place has become my own personal Eden, he thought. He would tell you right up front that he is a sterile engineer. He's not an engineer that works on sterile projects, and he is not a super clean man. It means he cannot father children, can't get anybody pregnant. When the mumps "fell on him," as the old folks say, it settled in his testicles. It became both a blessing and a curse, starting with his first visit to "The Crossroads Store" when he met her.

ABOUT THE AUTHOR

Allan Young is an Appalachian native, engineer, riverboat captain, newspaper and magazine editor, and writer of many books and stories set in his home area. He has first hand knowledge of the mountains. He understands the people, their loves, their hates, their fears, their joys, and their way of life—as well as what havoc change and turmoil can wreak on them.

THE HEAD ROCK CHALLENGE

Prologue, THE CALL TO RETURN

Jed hated her.

He hated her for bringing him into the world with only one good eye.

He hated her for the abuse she heaped upon him before he was six years old and they found out, at school, that he was blind in one eye—the beatings, the threats the constant fright.

He hated her for the beatings she administered to his brother Josh, which became worse after they found out about Jed's eye.

He hated Josh, too, for his confidence, his sound body, and, later, his pretty wife and good job—even the fact that Josh could be accepted by the Navy and Jed wasn't.

He hated her for the verbal abuse she laid on his two older sisters, the way she accused them of relationships with boys, opening and reading all their mail, and sometimes destroying it before they even saw it.

He hated her for the way she treated his father—always trying to drag him into her church, and actually hitting him for disagreeing with her.

And he hated her for worshipping the preachers, and caring more for the church members than her own family.

He hated her for interfering in his marriage, and blamed her in part for its ultimate failure.

He blamed her for turning his kids against him and hated her for becoming involved when he became convinced that the youngest wasn't his, and put him through the blood testing ordeal—which proved nothing.

She had given Jed life, and he hated her for that—spending most of his life wishing he had never been born.

And now she had sent for him. The call had come from his sister, Della.

"Mom hasn't got much time left, and she desperately wants to see you," she had said.

He had tried living in Kingsport, even moving his business there, to be close to her, and do his duty in looking after her, but she had interfered so much in his business and personal life that he had been forced to move back to Knoxville, just to put some distance between them.

And now here he was, driving back to Kingsport after all these years. But not directly. It was only about an hour and a half drive between the two cities, but he had chosen to take the roundabout route through Cumberland Gap and on up through Lee County, Jonesville, Pennington Gap, and across Wallins Ridge. Maybe he could get a different perspective, seeing his old boyhood home and the stomping grounds of his youth.

Just how did he get to where he was today, he wondered, as he rolled across the sunlit hills and valleys? It seemed to him that the harder he worked, the more life smote him. Nothing had ever come easy, although he was a fairly successful small businessman, others seemed to have all the luck—and a lot of his bad luck was brought on by others.

As he drove under the Head Rock, now renamed Stone Face, he recalled the time his brother and Bob Moore had climbed the Window Rock, up on Black Mountain. But he couldn't do it. Josh had always loved heights, but Jed was deathly afraid. He had stood longingly at the bottom and watched on many occasions while Josh and his friends had climbed every cliff in the county. Except one. They had never been able to climb the Head Rock—three hundred feet above the roaring river. Oh, they claimed they had once, but they had simply climbed the ridge behind the Rock, then worked their way out on top of it—not climbing the face at all. But he couldn't even do that.

As he again visited the empty building which once housed the restaurant where he met his wife, drove past the high school building, now a grade school, and past the old home at the base of Elk Knob, his reminisces caught up with him—and he started to relive his life as he saw it in the mountains and valleys of this long forgotten area.

Chapter 1, LOOKING BACK

Jed hated those damned little old coal camps he grew up in. He hated the dirt, the roadside trash, the creeks full of garbage, the dusty slate-based roads and most of all, the people. He didn't get claustrophobia—he didn't fear the mountains falling in on him, as his brother did, but he hated them just the same. Even when he was very young and his folks moved out in the valley a few miles away from the coal, he still felt the nearness of it, and saw the same trashiness and dirtiness. He never had to worry about working underground in them, he wasn't physically able to, but he hated them just the same—because he was trapped. He couldn't figure a way to get out, as his brother had.

So he escaped with his guitar, as he was doing today.

He sat on his sister's couch and strummed away, silently watching her do her housework. He knew this made her nervous, but he didn't care—her husband owned a much better guitar than he would ever be able to afford, and he loved to play it. So this he did whenever he had the opportunity, as he did this Saturday morning.

Reminiscing as he picked, he thought of his high school days, recently completed, when he graduated at the head of his class—as the valedictorian. And he really hadn't had to study too hard. When you don't have too many friends, and practically no activities, it's easier to remember the things necessary to get good scores on tests. Or was it just that there was no competition? Were the other members of his class just too stupid to make a showing? His mind told him this was probably the cause. He really didn't care.

He hadn't dated in high school—couldn't really see himself with any of those daffy little girls that he knew. And he avoided fights, which he had been unable to do in grade school. Seems like in the old Elk Knob School, which unfortunately burned down the year after he finished—unfortunate because for the prior six years he had hoped it would—he was always fighting. Usually to defend his brother, or somebody else set upon by more than one kid. Also he pounded a few kids for telling his mother lies about him—taught them a lesson—and for picking on a neighbor's kid who was retarded.

Quite often he had been standing before the principal defending himself, or at least explaining why he did what he did. And, much to the chagrin of his teachers and the principal, he always received good grades.

They had not known about his eye until he started school, and was tested for the first time. He had always seemed to turn his left eye in a little, people told him, but now they learned he was almost completely blind in it. Since, as a small child, he had always heard about how you had to be in good physical condition to get a job – the mines, the railroads, stores or government—he started to feel a little undesirable, as well as resentful. He would show them, he had thought, so he went through the first three grades in one year.

This feeling of weakness, he felt, probably made him less than attractive to the opposite sex, yet there had been some who seemed to be happy to be around him. The fortunate thing was that most of them were not too desirable either.

He had not avoided controversy, however, and when he was appointed editor of the high school newspaper, he had deliberately written editorials on subjects which the principal had discouraged him from attacking. Sometimes it made him friends, sometimes enemies. He really didn't care one way or the other.

Even with his eye problem, he had been able to get on at the local newspaper, and enjoyed publishing—although basically he was a flunky and errand boy. He wanted desperately to learn how to run the linotype machine to set type, but the old operator who ran it wouldn't teach him. The old guy, he guessed, was afraid Jed would take his job. Jed couldn't tell him that all he wanted was to get good enough at it to go somewhere and get a better job doing that.

Now, sitting here on Esther's couch, picking her husband's guitar, he remembered how he started this hobby and picked up this skill. One of his schoolmates, Ken, had had polio, which left one leg all shriveled up so he had to wear a heavy metal brace. Ken also had to put his hand on that knee to stabilize himself with each step. One day when Jed came back to Elk Knob School after going home for lunch, he walked over to a group of boys who seemed to be laughing and talking and having a lot of fun. As he approached he found out why. They had formed a ring around Ken and were, with great exaggeration, imitating the way he walked—then laughing like maniacs. Knowing who the ringleader of this particular group was, Jed coolly forced his way through the ring, cocked his fist, and blasted the kid right in the nose—his favorite place to hit people. The effect was instant—the blood and snot just flew, and the mob scattered.

"I'm going to tell the teacher!" screamed the ringleader.

"Go ahead," said Jed, "I'm sure she'll want to know why I hit you. Be sure to tell her that."

He didn't, of course.

Ken became his best, if not his only, follower. This used to bother him—him with his independent nature—until he found out Ken played the guitar. It stood to reason, a good kid who was kept out of physical activities because of his leg, would naturally gravitate to something else. Jed had always had musical leanings, but could not afford an instrument. Now he found himself at Ken's house as often as possible while Ken taught him how to play.

Brooding about his condition and relationships with other people had become the norm when he was plunking away in what to others looked like an absent-minded manner on the guitar, but today it seemed worse than usual. He laid the guitar back in on his sister's bed, where it was kept, without a case, since it never left the house, and he got up and strolled out the front door without saying a word, and off down the road towards home, a half mile away.

As he casually entered the house through the kitchen door, his mother met him with a piece of paper in her hand. Her brown eyes were flashing, and her face was beet red.

"This is from that little bitch you've been shackin' up with," she said, "I told you to stop seeing trash. That's how your cousin got killed. She's nothing but trash, and now she's pregnant!"

"Gimme that,'" he reached for the paper, "What are you doing reading my mail anyway. You're always doin' that, and it's none of your business."

"No, you can't have it. And I'll read anything that comes on this place. You're still my son, and I'm not going to let you go to hell full of sins of the flesh!" she screamed.

Then she slapped him right across the eyes. And she continued slapping him with first one hand then the other.

The hate swelled up in Jed until it overpowered him. The hate for her, for his life, for where he lived, for his job—and he did something he never thought he would do. He grabbed his mother around the neck, his fingers closing tight, and threw her backwards on the kitchen table on her back.

His hands shutting off her screams, he said slowly and coolly, "If you ever get in my way again, Old Woman, I'll kill you. And I just might right now."

Letting her go, he reached for the letter, and while she gasped for breath, read it to himself. Yes, he had dated this girl a couple of times. No, he was not and had not "shacked up" with her. When her boyfriend came home from the Army they had gotten engaged, and yes, she was getting married, and she was pregnant. That's what the letter was about. Silently, he wished her well. Whoever her new mother-in-law was would be a better one than she would have had with him.

"Your Daddy will kill you when I tell him about this," she was saying.

"No, he'll probably thank me, considering the way you have been treating him for the past few years. Mom, I'm sorry I had to get rough with you, but it's been a long time coming. Don't ever make me have to do it again. I might lose control."

"I don't see why you can't be as nice as your brother," she cried through tears of fright and disgust. "Josh never would have treated his mother like this."

"Of course not," he said. "He went away to keep from it. Someone else in his shoes would have killed you and the Old Man both by now. He just walked away from it all—something I can't do. I envy him. And you know what? He's found a nice Catholic girl there in Ohio. He'll marry her—he hates these hills anyway—and you'll never see him again!"

Chapter 2, JOSH

Jed didn't know whether he hated his brother, Josh, or not—he never thought about it one way or another. They had nothing in common, didn't even like the same kind of music. He hated to admit it, even to himself, but he envied Josh—maybe he always had. He hadn't envied the beatings and verbal abuse the folks heaped on Josh, especially after they found out Jed had only one good eye. They fairly well left Jed alone, apparently regretting that they had created an imperfect child. Well, hadn't they?

He and Josh had gotten along reasonably well when they were little kids because of their interest in the outdoors. They had shared many happy days on Elk Knob and the Buzzard Roost, as well as on the banks of the river or in their old flat bottomed skiff. Of course, because of his folks' sympathy for him and his handicap, he had been able to milk them for things Josh never had. He had gotten a store bought coaster wagon, something Josh never had, except the ones their father made, and an air rifle, which Josh would have given anything for—but they wouldn't let Josh have anything until Jed was big enough for it, and by then Josh was too big. The same way with bicycles. Josh finally talked them into going into debt for a new bicycle for him, then that same summer they bought Jed a used one, which turned out to be too heavy for him, so they made Josh trade him his new one for it.

He also convinced them to buy him a new catcher's mitt and face mask, after they decided to let him play baseball only as a catcher, and only if he never took his mask off to go after the ball. Josh had traded some kid a knife for an old glove. Josh always made out, and complained very little.

Jed was really happy at first when the Old Man landed on Josh with his mining belt when the two boys were playing mumble-peg and Josh slid the knife across the floor where Jed brought his foot down on the open blade. It wasn't Josh's fault, but Jed hurt so much and was so frightened at seeing so much of his own blood that initially he was glad to see Josh being hurt for it. This led to fright and fear for Josh when it seemed like the Old Man didn't know when to stop. Josh cried and screamed, then sulked for several days, but offered no resistance. Jed figured he thought that was just the way things were.

His and Josh's outdoor adventures were expanded by the acquisition of bicycles. Now they were not limited to the backwoods and rivers, but could reach some of the other towns, as well. Of course, Josh put his to good use by getting a job as a stable boy and gardener for an old farm couple with no children who lived a couple of miles away. His brother's regular income was something else for Jed to envy.

As they went on into high school, Josh seemed to be surrounded by friends his own age, and seemed to have no trouble getting close to the prettiest girls—not the prom queen types, but the real sincere beauties who were nice to be around.

Now there he was up in Dayton, engaged to the most beautiful girl either of then had ever seen—a revelation which sent his mother through the roof!

While Josh had been in the Navy, a move which Jed could not possibly make, Jed had had so many run-ins with Mr. Bender, the high school principal, that Bender tried every way in the world to keep him from being the class valedictorian—but there was no one anywhere near him gradewise. Again, just stupid kids, he thought.

He got his revenge when the year ended and it came time to dispose of the earnings of the school newspaper. His brother had purchased a plaque listing all the graduates who were killed in the military, plus several hundred dollars worth of chemical laboratory equipment, when he was editor two years before. On the last day of school, gleefully remembering that he and the principal had argued over a lot of things, and that his brother Josh had been paddled by Bender his last year of school, Jed called in his two closest friends, who were press staff members, and divided up the money—two for him, and one for each of them!

A few weeks out of school, and finding out that he couldn't work for his father, he had tried to follow in his brother's footsteps by taking off for Dayton and finding a job. Not getting hired in a factory, where the money was, because of his eye, he had to settle for a position shuffling papers in an office. Since it paid only two thirds what the factory paid, it was a letdown. Although it was better than nothing, he started to think more and more of doing something on his own—where his eye would have no effect. Besides, the lifestyle of his brother and his friends didn't suit him anyway.

He had started checking around and found out that the barber colleges in Tennessee had only an eight-week course—then you could get licensed. There had been a time in high school when he cut hair, anyway. The neighborhood country barber always took a break and went to church on Saturday night, so whoever showed up for a trim just waited—his shop was always open. One night when the place was full and Jed was there, he announced that he thought he could cut hair, and some guy said he could cut his—he was in a hurry. So this became a regular Saturday night schedule, Jed cutting hair while the barber went to church.

Now he was considering it as a profession—hence the return home to the job at the newspaper, in order live at home and save enough money to head for Knoxville.

Josh came back once during this time, when their father died. Jed didn't understand why he couldn't have been there when it happened, but he wasn't. Why did he always feel left out?

Chapter 3, NORMA

Jed saw her almost every day, and they had become friends. She was a waitress at the restaurant where he ate lunch—reasonably attractive and easy to talk to. Since he went to lunch later than most people in town, he was usually one of the few people in the restaurant at that time, so they got acquainted. She was not pushy, and seemed to accept his reluctance to talk about himself with no problem. Her name, he learned, was Norma.

One evening he found himself in town late, so after work he went back up to the restaurant. He was still there when she started to put on her coat. On the spur of the moment he approached her.

"I'll drive you home," he said, and she quietly agreed.

After chatting for a while on her front porch, and making no further plans, he drove on home. It didn't occur to him to consider whether he wanted to see her again or not.

The next day when he went up for lunch, he didn't see her there, and didn't ask about her, presuming she was ill or maybe it was just her day off. It didn't matter to him. The following day she was back at work, and for a girl who usually wore very little makeup, she was heavily made up and wearing dark glasses. Suspecting what the problem was, he said nothing, but went back about closing time. Catching up with her as she tried to sneak out the back door, he reached for her arm.

"Not tonight," she said.

"Your father?" he asked.

"Yes," she answered. "He saw you bring me home the other night. He was drunk."

"Does he work?" Jed asked.

"No, and I have two little brothers. My mother is dead."

"I'm going home with you," he stated flatly.

"O.K. But not to the door."

She made him park quite a way from the house, and when she got out of the car she was standing on a small embankment beside the road leading up to her house—still wearing the dark glasses, although darkness had set in. Walking up to her, the embankment made her the same height as him, so, slipping his right hand under her dark hair on her neck, he pulled her towards him and gently kissed her on her bruised lips.

"Oh, my," she said. "Now I don't know what to do, except say goodnight."

As she walked up to her house he stood there watching her go, thinking that she might not know what to do, but he sure as hell did! He followed her.

Just as he reached the porch, she closed the door behind her, and he heard the smack of a fist hitting flesh, then heard her scream. Kicking the door open, he saw her lying on the floor, sunglasses askew and blood running from a cut on her already bruised cheek. Cowering in a corner of the room were boys about eight and ten, and standing over her with a glazed look in is eyes was a stocky, bow-legged, balding man of about forty five who was starting to talk to her about "doing that again."

Jed heard ribs crack as he punched the man as hard as he could in the left side. When the man raised his right arm to strike, Jed grabbed it and brought it down behind the man's back in a severe twisting motion and heard both bones break in the forearm. Then he spun the man around facing him for the first time, and saw the fear in his eyes, as he fully realized the hate in Jed's. Jed, using his favorite punch as a small boy, hit the man full in the face, feeling the nose collapse beneath his fist, and seeing the blood start to flow freely.

By now the man was lying on the floor crying and moaning that he was dying. Jed stood over him.

Looking over at Norma, who by now had dragged herself up on a couch where she and the two boys were sobbing beyond control, he asked, "Your father?"

She and the boys nodded numbly.

Looking down at the man, Jed addressed him for the first time.

"I'm Jed Allen," he said, "and you are going to see a lot of me around here. If you ever lay a hand on her—or these boys—again, this is just a sample of what you'll get. Now let's get you to the hospital. You can tell them you got drunk and got in a bar fight. It's not too far from the truth."

From then on the old man stayed pretty well off the sauce, and eventually got religion. He ran around behind Jed seeing what he could do to help him out—subservient almost to the point of embarrassment.

While at barber college, Jed came up every weekend to see Norma.

His eight weeks in Knoxville were uneventful, and he came out with a barber's license—although one still wasn't required in his home state. He cut hair in Pennington for a while, then found a better job in Appalachia, where the coal mines were going full strength and there were more men needing haircuts.

After finishing school and getting into a steady job, it stood to reason that he and Norma would get married. It was a quiet wedding, with no fanfare, and no disagreements with the parents of either of them. Neither of them, Jed or Norma, liked pomp and circumstance, so many people who knew them as individuals did not even know they were married.

For the first time, Jed felt like he was accepted, and had some things of his own. He was happy with Norma, and was considered a good barber at the shop where he worked.

Chapter 4, MIGRATION

Norma's father had proved a real boon to Jed after he bought a house and put a barber shop in it. He was working five days a week at the Appalachia shop, then cutting hair at home nights and days off if anybody showed up. This left him little time for work around the house, and maintenance or remodeling chores. That's where the father-in-law came in. His respect, or fear, of Jed hadn't faded, and even though Jed still hated him for what he had done to Norma when he thought he was going to lose his meal ticket, and he still couldn't hold a job, he worked like a slave for Jed. He did everything asked, plus a lot of things voluntarily, to keep their home in order.

But, by the time his two sons were old enough to join the Army, his years of drinking caught up with him, and once he got sick he didn't last long. Now, as far as her immediate family was concerned, Norma was alone. She had worked at the courthouse almost ever since she married Jed, but now a cutback in staff was leaving her jobless.

When she told Jed, he took it lightly.

"Now's a good time to find greener pastures," he said.

So a few months later found them in Baltimore—where they had seen friends move to over the years.

Although they fell in with some other country musicians whom they enjoyed very much, the Maryland city did not turn out to be too lucrative jobwise.

When some other acquaintances who lived in Detroit found out they were heading away from home, they had encouraged them to come there. Then they had sent Jed information on the price of haircuts, so when the first venture didn't work out, they simply drove on to Michigan.

Renting an apartment in the same building as some other people from their home area, Jed trekked on down to the courthouse to get his barber's license. A short time later a very dejected barber was trudging home to his wife again—to give her the bad news. You had to be a resident for six months before you could be licensed to cut hair anywhere in Michigan. Protectionism!

Then good luck caught up with him. As he approached the apartment building where they had taken up residence, he spotted a sign which appealed to him.

"Help Wanted," it said, "Printing Experience Helpful But Not Necessary." It was in the window of a print shop right in his neighborhood!

"I can do anything except run a linotype," he said, when he entered and asked for the job, "and I know how it works. I can start now."

"Then we'll teach you that," said the owner. "Welcome aboard!"

Here was the solution to his immediate employment problem, and it was doing something he liked to do anyway.

So they settled into a big city way of life, and even after he got his license to barber, he still put in a little time at the printer's, just to keep his hand in. What he disliked the most about the city, although he both lived and worked in a residential area, was the tavern habitués. Some people just couldn't get home from work without stopping off at the tavern for one, or two or more. Some of them never got home for supper, and weren't even expected. Jed's money came too hard for him to drink it up.

As the years went on, though, and they were able to afford better furniture and a better car, Norma started to talk more about home—home being back in the mountains. He ignored it for a while, then it became obsessive with her, and finally, they had a quarrel over it. He could not impart to her his hatred of the hills, the lack of opportunity because of his eye—which he had almost forgotten about in his current profession, as well as his sideline.

With the demise of the coal mines, or at least with the greatly mechanized mining methods that used fewer men, there just weren't enough men in the area to get haircuts. It was bad enough in Detroit, with more and more younger men wearing long hair. A barber had to be located where there were still a lot of World War II types who still believed in short, neat hair. And for now, a place of many factory workers, like Detroit, was it.

But Norma kept it up, she would wistfully look at old photographs of the mountains, then ask him to compare that to the view out of their apartment windows—views of other apartments. And they quarreled more, and they made up more.

Then, when both of her brothers were discharged from the Army and headed home, it was more than she could take. She had to go home. Still his stubbornness and taciturn behavior won out—he simply wouldn't discuss it. The quarreling by her got louder, the nagging became more aggressive—and of course, the making up became more loving.

Then one day she met him at the door with some startling news—that which they had hoped for, at least to some degree all these years was finally come true, they were going to be parents!

"And we don't want to raise our baby here, do we?" she cried through tears of joy.

"No," he told her, "I'll figure something out."

"It should be easy," he thought. "Hell, after all, I did get elected to membership in the Mensa Society, an organization of people with I.Q.'s over 160. So I should be able to figure out how to make a living in the mountains—and keep it legal."

So, within two months, he had everything in place, and they were shaking the grime of Detroit from their shoes.

Chapter 5, HOME BUSINESS

His idea for being a success back in the hills, since it looked like that's where he had to be in order to have any peace at home, was to try to continue doing exactly what he was doing in Detroit, and that was to cut hair and print things. He was able to find a building which he could purchase rather reasonably, right on the main drag, which had suitable living quarters upstairs and an area for a business down.

He set up his barber shop in the front of the place, and then, behind a wall, set up a print shop. With what little money he had been able to save during the Detroit years he was able to buy an old platen type of letterpress for printing, plus a variety of type, which he could set by hand. He was ready for business, and specialized in handbills, letterheads, envelopes and other simple printed business matter. The work for either of his businesses didn't exactly come flooding in, but he and Norma were happy.

She was happy to be "back home," where she felt more secure, and he was happy because the quarreling and nagging has ceased, or at least dropped to a minimum. It was there that their son was born.

As Jed struggled along trying to eke out a living, two truths became evident. He didn't get much printing business walking in off the street, and when he went out and made calls, something he hated to do anyway, that seemed to be when barbering customers came in, so he missed them. He would have liked to move both businesses to a larger town, even a few miles away, but Norma wouldn't hear of it. So sometimes they quarreled when he brought it up.

Then much to his surprise, she found out she was expecting their second child. Here they had been married all those years with no children, and in the space of two years she was pregnant twice. They had never questioned why they were unable to have children earlier. They had just accepted it, since being parents was a hope, but not an obsession with either of them, anyway. They had never bothered to go through any tests or even discuss it with their doctors.

But now, with the family growing, he needed more income, and felt that he had to do something to expand one or both businesses. The printing could be the most lucrative, since he had actually had to turn down business because his equipment couldn't handle it. Besides, his old letterpress required a lot of maintenance, something he had experienced, and hated, in his father's business. If only he could find a way to acquire more and better printing equipment—but there was no way he could come up with that much money. He had none, and wasn't earning enough to save any.

He did no business with banks, and always dealt in cash, so he had not become friends, or familiar with any local bankers. But he decided to try his luck anyway. The first one he talked to laughed at him, the second said he needed a better business "prospectus" than he had, whatever that was, and the third did at least encourage him by suggesting that he get another property owner to cosign a loan. When he offered to put his place up for collateral, the banker pointed out that he owed much more on it than it was worth. He started to realize how much he hated bankers! If you can go to them and convince them that you don't need any money, then they will loan you all kinds of it—otherwise, don't bother them, unless you want to be laughed at.

He started to look at offset equipment anyway, and visited other print shops to see how their equipment worked, by pretending to be a potential customer. After selecting the exact press he thought he would like to have, plus all the needed paraphernalia to put it to work, it became an obsession with him. He even thought about stealing the money, but he had no idea who might have enough. He carried the catalog around in his hip pocket and looked at it from time to time, just like a kid dreaming about a new bicycle.

Although his mother had disapproved of his marriage to

Norma—hell, she disapproved of everything and everybody—she had come around after the baby was born, and now came to help with the second one, also a boy. One day he heard her ask Norma what he was so grumpy about.

Norma said, “He wants to buy some printing machine, and can’t get the money.”

Whereupon his mother chimed in, “Why don’t he go get a job somewhere, like his brother?”

With that, he turned on her.

“Because I’m not like my brother, remember? You made him whole, but you left part of me out!”

Then it hit him. Here was a property owner who could cosign his bank loan. The old home place was clear—all paid for—his dad paid cash for it. Besides, it was one-eighth his anyway, if she and his siblings ever agreed to sell it. His dad had left it half to his mother and the other half to the four kids in equal shares.

While his mother was put out by his last remark, he knew this was a good time to hit her up for it. She didn’t understand it right away, and told him she didn’t have any money.

After he explained the cosign bit, she said, “You mean all I have to do is sign to back you up, but you pay them back?”

“Yes,” he assured her, “and with the new equipment, I won’t have any trouble making the payments at the bank.”

But he was wrong. There still was not enough business to keep it alive and make the payments, and within six months of procurement of the press, he couldn’t make the payment. By the end of the first year, his mother was screaming at him about the letters she was getting from the bank about taking the home place. He assured her that they couldn’t because she was not the only owner.

And he was wrong again!

The bank representative knew that the will was written so that she could sell the place without the permission of her children, then distribute the proceeds to the other four owners.

Jed wasn't even bothered when his mother told him the bank had scheduled an auction sale of the property.

"So what," he thought, *"I've got my press, and now I'll get my share of the sale price. She doesn't need it anyway. She doesn't even live there."*

He was delighted when he learned that his sister and her husband wanted to buy the place—delighted that his mother wouldn't sell it to them.

"They don't deserve it," he chuckled to himself.

Jed didn't go to the sale, but was disappointed when he heard that the lady who said she was going to buy it as an investment backed down when some young man bid on it. She had told him since he needed a home she wouldn't take it away from him. Jed became even more upset when told that it took both his share and his mother's to pay off the bank, so neither of them got anything from the sale.

Then when he found out that the young man who bought it was a relative of his sister's husband, and was buying it for them, he became furious. This fury became a screaming tantrum at Norma and his mother, when she told him that his brother and his other sister had endorsed their checks over to their mother. She came out all right, he got nothing, and his siblings were embarrassing and tormenting him from hundreds of miles away.

Lord, how he hated these people!

Chapter 6, JEALOUSY

It was finally coming home to Jed that his location was licking him, and, as much as he hated to, he was going to have to start commuting again. He had never liked driving to Appalachia to work as a barber before their sojourn in Michigan, and now it would be even worse if he were working at two businesses where he never knew when he would get finished. Working at home was easy, he cut hair when someone showed up, and he printed when he had something to print. But there hadn't been enough of either to keep them going, and there would be no more loans. He had to go where there was traffic.

He would have much preferred just packing up and moving to another larger town, Kingsport, Knoxville, Bristol—somewhere like that. But he knew he would have a battle royal on his hands if he did. This was home to Norma, and there was nothing he could do about it. But he couldn't see just sitting here hoping things would get better while they starved either. Soon those boys would be in school—what then? He had to admit that for the last few years, even though times had been tough, he and Norma had been getting along very well, until the press episode started preying on his thinking and his normal withdrawn demeanor had changed to an occasionally explosive one.

She loved this place, and he began hating it more and more. Hating it economically, hating it domestically and hating it for what it was doing to his thinking. So, when in Big Stone picking up a print job he discovered that space in an old storefront was for rent at a reasonable rate, he took it. Here were miners from the surrounding areas, business people from three different towns, new highway construction through there, and many more people and businesses of all types than he would ever see where he was now. They would still live there, but he would drive the fifteen miles back and fourth.

When he told her, Norma didn't like it, of course, but the deal was done. After he made the move, he realized that before, working at home, he had filled in his idle moments with the kids, or on home projects, and now he couldn't do that. But, at the same time, he had more time to read, study printing methods and even do a little writing, something he had never really done much of. But his business did pick up, and his income showed it right away. He was putting in many hours, and many seven day weeks, and really missed being home more, but the income was worth it.

However, when he was home, he noticed Norma's two brothers, now out of the Army, hanging around more and more, and they were always there for supper when he was. He knew they weren't too "work brickle," as his father used to say, but had always been able to make out on odd jobs, unemployment, welfare—whatever came their way. They had pretty well stayed away from him, probably thinking he would put them to work as he had their father before he died. But now, not only were they there when he came home but he suspected they were there when he was not, since Norma seemed to need more and more money for groceries—and she and the two boys couldn't possibly be eating that much.

While coping with these situations as best he could, he had started to dig into the printing business more, since more men were going the long hair route, and the barber shop was sometimes a waste of space. He had seen an ad in a magazine for submissions of poetry, which it said would be printed free in hard cover books. Since he had published a few poems during his high school days as editor, he rounded up a few of them, typed copies and sent them in. Back came a form letter of acceptance, and a solicitation for him to buy one or more of the books.

"I could do that," he said to himself, "publish books and sell them to the authors of the contributed material."

He had no idea at the time, but running his first small classified advertisement was to start him on a lifelong career of which he had no prior knowledge at all.

Everybody in the world things he's a damned poet, he thought, as the returns on the ad came thick and fast.

Pretty soon he was on to his second, then his third book, and didn't have time for either cutting hair or doing print jobs for other people. He worked all day and half the night on his books.

Her name was Beverly, and he hired her from a want ad he ran in the local paper. He just couldn't keep up with the work, and the money was coming in fine, since he waited until he had all the books sold, and cash in hand, before he ever produced one. So he could afford some help, and besides, the more books he could produce, the more money he would make.

Norma blew up.

"I don't want you working in an office with that woman," she said. "I'll hire a babysitter and I'll do your work—I'll help you."

"Now, you know you don't want someone else raising these boys, and I don't either," he reiterated, "besides, Bev is probably just the first of many employees, if it grows the way I think and hope it will."

"I won't have you working with a room full of women," she screamed, reminiscent of his mother.

He tried to point out to her that it was in an open office, with big plate glass windows in front, and there was no reason to be jealous. To the best of his knowledge, she had never been jealous before, and he hadn't either, although he used to burn a little when they were together, before and after they were married, when she would greet some former restaurant customer in an unusually friendly manner.

Every night when he came home it started all over again, so he was losing sleep while fighting business problems and personal ones too. Finally, he brought up the subject of her brothers.

"If we are complaining about the way we are living, and our relationships with other people," he said, "what about those two louts that I find asleep in our living room whenever I come home? And eating better than I do. We can't keep on feeding those lazy bums. You've got to tell them that."

"They're my brothers," she said, "and I'll feed them if I want to. They'll eat here as long as I have even one potato. They are family."

"But they are grown men," said Jed. "You might be cooking the food, but my hard-earned dollars are paying for it."

"You heard me," she said, "they're family, and I'll take care of them before I will you, you and your office full of sluts!"

That weekend Jed packed most of his clothes, went to a furniture company and bought a single bed which he put in the back room of his business office, and moved in. He didn't know if he would ever go home again.

Of course, as soon as his mother found out about it, she came screaming into his office.

"What about the kids?" she asked. "You should stay together because of them."

"Not when all their father and mother do is stand and scream at each other in front of them," he said.

"Well," she growled, "your dad and I never did get along, but I stayed with him because of you kids."

"Yeah, and all four kids kept wishing to hell you wouldn't. You were miserable, he was miserable and all us kids were even more miserable—and still are, because of it!" Jed shouted.

The look of disbelief in her eyes was satisfaction enough. Jed pushed her out and locked the door behind her.

Chapter 7, BREAKUP

Jed went along building his new business on a steady day-to-day basis, and adding employees as needed, until he had four more people besides Bev—three women and one man. The man didn't work out. Jed tried to teach him some of the physical jobs, which he alone had been doing, but the guy just made too many costly mistakes. He had to be let go.

Bev, of course, had been his mainstay ever since he hired her. He couldn't afford to pay any of them much more than minimum wage, but he tried to do a little better by her. Whenever he felt any emotion for her at all, it was sympathy. He literally felt sorry for her. She had no income except what he paid her, and she had three kids to support. She had a no-good ex-husband somewhere, but he never helped her at all, or ever came to see the kids. She lived in a rental mobile home, and couldn't afford a car of any kind—she walked to work from somewhere over on the backside of Imboden Hill.

She had never pried into his affairs, and her surprise didn't even show when Jed moved his bed into the back room of the office and started staying there nights. He didn't talk about his personal life at work, and she didn't either, although she did occasionally take her coffee break at the same time as he did, and join him to discuss business problems.

He was doing fairly well financially, and quit stewing about Norma supporting her brothers—at least on the outside. He still couldn't understand her thinking, which only encouraged them to be lazier. Well, at least she wasn't buying their clothes or giving them spending money. And, with two big healthy grown men hanging out at her house, at least she would be safe. No one would break in and bother her and the kids. He saw the kids as much as possible, usually on Sundays, and tried to get them off to himself as much as he could.

And he tended to indulge them too, in lieu of being able to be with them more. When Craig, the oldest, wanted a go-cart, he got him one. When they both, especially Tommy, the younger one, wanted a pony, he not only got him one, but had a small barn built on the back of their property and stocked it with hay. In order that they could be well dressed and comfortable, he was providing Norma with a good income. His business had prospered, and he was happy to share it with his family—even though it was impossible to share their lives.

His mother still needled him whenever she could, of course, about living apart, but he tried to ignore her. Being lonely, he found himself chatting with Bev a little more sometimes about his kids and their activities.

Then one spring day he passed by his old home and didn't see the pony anywhere. On subsequent trips by, it looked like no livestock was using the barn or lot. So, seeing the boys out playing one trip, he stopped and asked them about it.

"Mommy sold it," they said, "or Uncle Vernon did."

Fuming, he went storming into the house. Jumping up off the couch where she was watching television, Norma yelled, "You can't come barging in here like that. I'll have you arrested for trespassing."

"Trespassing, hell," he said, "don't forget you and I are married, and in the eyes of the law, this is my home. I have as much right here as anybody. Now what did you do with the boys' pony?"

"I sold it. I needed the money worse than they needed a pony."

"I'm sending you all kinds of money," he said. "Isn't it enough?"

"Vernon's getting married," she said, "and he needed a new suit."

"Oh, lord," he thought, *"now I'll be supporting his wife, too."*

He stalked out of the house, stopping to talk to the boys again.

"If your mom sells anything else I get you, be sure to let me know," he said.

"She sold my go-cart," said Craig. "Said both our uncles needed new suits for the wedding."

By now Jed was so mad he couldn't see straight, so he sat in his car for a few minutes before attempting to drive back to Big Stone.

I hate her, he thought, *I hate her more every day. I'll always hate her, maybe I always have. The very idea of caring more for those bums, leeches living off her—no, off me—than she does for me and the boys!*

He was under such a cloud all next day at the office that everybody stayed out of his way—even Bev. After everyone else left, she was still there. Fixing them both a cup of strong all-day coffee, she came into his semi-office—it had walls on three sides only.

"Want to talk about it?" she asked.

"No," he said. "It's none of your business."

"I know that," she said, "but I'm here to listen if you've got a story. It might help just to tell somebody."

They had worked together for over two years, and had never discussed personal matters, nor had they asked personal questions before.

"What went wrong with your marriage?" he asked, suddenly.

"I had an affair," she said totally surprising him.

He just couldn't imagine her having an affair.

"What went wrong with yours?"

"You had a what?" he asked in shocked disbelief.

"An affair. You want to hear about it? It's just one woman's story."

"Go ahead," he said.

"Well, as you have guessed," she started out, "my husband is and was a drunk. He never hurt me or the kids, he just drank. It cost him several jobs. He came home every night drunk, then drank some more. I tried to stop him, but you know how that is.

"Sometimes he couldn't come home, and I would have to get someone to stay with the kids and go looking for him in all the ditches and the jail. This went on for years. Except for being stubborn and doing just the opposite of what I wanted, and being totally remote from me personally, his drinking didn't affect me. But I worried.

"We got so poor that I took a part-time job as a waitress in a local restaurant. That's where I met him, the guy, after a year or so. He was a salesman of mining machinery, and he came in for supper every other Friday. Since he arrived late and stayed later, we talked quite a bit after everybody else left. Then one night he drove me home.

"As time went on, we got closer and closer, until I decided this had to stop before it led to trouble. So I told him to come to my house for a last and final goodbye talk. The kids were in school, and lord knows where my husband was, but he never came home in the daytime anyway.

"When my friend arrived, he was obviously nervous about being in my home. After a few minutes he suggested that we get in his car and go somewhere else to talk—so I went along.

"I thought we might drive up on the hill, or out in the country, or even to the East Stone airport. But the next thing I knew we were at a motel, where he said he had a room. I refused to go in, but he insisted he had no physical ideas at all, and we would have privacy to talk. So I went in.

"Well, you guessed it—we did more than just talk. And we kept doing it for three years."

"Why?" asked Jed.

"I was just so pleased to have someone of my own," she said, "someone who didn't drink, who was good to me, who was nice looking and who dressed well. Things I wasn't used to."

"Was he married?" asked Jed.

"I suspected that he was. But we never discussed it. Nor did we discuss my marriage."

"What broke it up?" asked Jed. "You said it lasted over three years."

"I found out I wasn't the only one. Just overheard a conversation at the restaurant. He denied it at first, then admitted it. I've seen him since from a distance. He's still around."

"So your husband found out and kicked you out?" Jed asked.

"Oh, no," she said, "he never knew. After this was all over I kicked him out, too. I sure didn't need a philanderer and a drunken bum. So I got rid of both of them. That's why I'm so glad to be working here. I know I'm not, but I sort of feel like I'm second in command, and it helped me get my pride back."

"I'm glad to be of help," he said, "and thanks for telling me the story."

"Now what about you?" she asked. "Just what went wrong with your life?"

"I found yours hard to believe at first," Jed said, "but I do believe it now. But I'm afraid you wouldn't believe mine at all."

Chapter 8, WIPEOUT

Jed put off telling Bev about his and Norma's troubles, although something deep inside told him that eventually he would. Since her own life's confession to him he started to look at her differently. He still felt sorry for her, but now there was a certain amount of admiration too. Here was a woman who had literally reached down and grabbed herself by her bootstraps and started pulling. And she wasn't bitter, or blaming others, or living so much in the past. She was simply trying to do better. And he began to appreciate the way she caught on to his type of work more and more and could do her part independently.

After finding that Norma had sold his kids' possessions in order to finance her brother's wedding, he quit sending her any money at all, forcing her to go to court to get support payments out of him. She knew what his reported income was, because as a married couple, they still filed a joint income tax return. He made it out and she simply signed it, since she had no other income.

On their day to appear in front of the judge, she showed up in a ragged dress, run-down shoes and stringy hair. For a woman who usually looked as neat as a pin, Jed was ashamed of her, but he knew what she was up to.

"Now I know you plan to tell the judge what my true income is, not what it says on the return. If you do they will get me for tax evasion. You know that," he said, when he met her in the courthouse corridor.

"Good," she said, emphatically, "I'd like to see you behind bars. Maybe they'll just lock you up while we are here!"

"You, too," Jed said, just as emphatically, "remember those are your tax returns, too. It's your income, your signature. Whatever happens to me, happens to you."

Norma's jaw dropped. Suddenly, he realized, all her plans were shot to hell. She had come to court to expose him, and go away with a big income assignment from him, and now even she was smart enough to know she couldn't do it without jeopardizing herself, too. The judge's payment assignment, based on Jed's reported income, was less than twenty-five percent of what he had been giving her—and he had been paying for things for the boys besides.

Well, Jed told himself, he would not let them starve, and he would certainly see to it that the boys were well dressed and had everything they needed for school. But, he hoped, this would end her feeding her brothers, now that she had to do a little budgeting.

When he stopped by the house later it was after school and the boys were out playing.

Craig was watching a small motorcycle go by when Jed asked, "Ever rode one of them?"

"No," they both said, "but we'd like to."

"I'll tell you what," said Jed, "I'll get one, which we can all ride, but I'll keep it at my place, and you can ride it when you are there."

The boys thought that was fine.

Going in the house, he picked up the mail out of the box and absent-mindedly looked through it as he walked. To his surprise there was a letter addressed to Norma from somebody in the Army. He opened it and read one of the mushiest love letters he had ever seen!

On impulse, he started digging through some dresser drawers until he found what he was looking for—a little red chest which he had gotten Norma for her birthday many years before. In it were several more letters of the same type, and photos of a man in uniform, some of which included Norma, and some were taken of them with the bride and groom at Vernon's wedding.

"What are you doing?" asked Norma, in a high-pitched voice, from the doorway. "Gimme those. You have no right to those!"

Jed started laughing uncontrollably.

"Is this the best you can do for a boyfriend? I'm your husband, and I can go through my own dresser drawers, can't I? I think I'll take these with me. They'll go over good in divorce court. Just how long has this been going on, anyway?"

"You'll never know!" she shouted, eyes blazing. "Get out of my house, and if you ever come back, me and my brothers will kill you!"

Shaking his head from side to side, and chuckling, he took the chest and headed for his car.

She might have been serious, he thought. *Her brothers are sneaky. They might even set fire to my business. Have to be careful.*

When he arrived back at the office, Bev met him with some bad news—all three of the other girls had resigned. The federal government was starting an office training school in the area, and for going to school twenty hours per week, would pay them two-thirds as much as he paid them for forty hours. The classes lasted sixteen weeks.

He called all three of them in his office and was told this was too good to pass up.

"What are you going to do at the end of the sixteen weeks?"

"Why, come back to work," one said.

"Not here. And where are you going to find a job? None of you had worked for a long time when I hired you. There aren't any jobs."

Well, they told him collectively, they would give it a try.

Asking Bev about what her plans were later, the answer he received pleased him—she said she was here to stay.

"Let's go eat," he said. "We can make some plans over lunch."

He had often thought that if his business volume ever dropped off, he would try to operate with just himself and Bev, and if there were fluctuations, maybe he could farm out part of the work. Suddenly he was faced with that choice, whether he wanted to or not. He figured all the other available typists in the area would be attending that stupid school, too.

When he approached Bev about it at lunch, she enthusiastically endorsed the plan. Again she assured him she had no plans beyond what she was doing. Somehow he felt closer to her, suddenly, than he had ever felt to any woman, even Norma. With Norma it had been her mistreatment by her father that had brought then together in the first place, but here was a woman who really was interested in him as him. She wanted to see him succeed, and wanted to be part of that success.

"Well," he said, teasingly, "now that we have the future of the business ironed out, you might as well tell me that you love me, so we can go back to work."

Looking him right in the eye, she really surprised him by saying, slowly and deliberately, "I do love you, Jed, and I have ever since I met you. But I still don't know the status of your marriage."

Somehow all she said made sense.

"I'll tell you tonight," he said.

They spent the rest of the afternoon planning and scheduling how they could finish the projects already in the mill, and start the new ones—without the other three staff members. They worked until long after dark.

Volunteering to drive Norma home, Jed took a long way around Imboden Hill and pulled off in a roadside park, where they sat quietly watching the moon come up over the eastern ridges.

"Did you mean it?" he finally asked.

"With all my heart!" she exclaimed.

With that they were in each other's arms, and soon he was learning how a front loader bra hooked—something he had never seen before.

After awhile, as they were straightening themselves up, she whispered, “I don’t believe I did that, and in a car with my boss. I hadn’t done that at all in over four years.”

“It’s been longer than that for me,” Jed said. “And don’t think of me as your boss. We’re partners—and you’re second in command, remember!”

Chapter 9, JOSH AGAIN

After he bought the motorcycle, which he kept right in his office work area, and notified the boys of it, Jed went by their house one Sunday afternoon and saw them outside. He stopped and picked them up and took them to his office. At fourteen, Craig was old enough to get a license to ride a lightweight motorcycle, but at twelve, Tommy wasn’t legal—but he was a big kid. So Jed let him ride anyway. Later that evening he took the boys home, to be met at the gate by a very upset Norma.

“Where have you been with my sons,” she screamed, “you’re going to get them killed!”

“They are my sons, too,” he said quietly, “and I’ll treat them nice whenever I can.”

“They’re not your sons,” she said, “they never were! And now you’re not my husband, either!”

The latter part was true. He didn’t feel right being with Bev while still married to Norma, even if it had been six years since they lived together, and Bev had been sharing his bed in the back room quite regularly now. Then, too, his income had climbed so rapidly with his staff reduction that he didn’t want Norma to know how much he really was making.

He had learned that, in his area, if a married couple hasn’t cohabited in over two years, divorce is automatic, all you have to do is get someone to sign an affidavit to the effect that you haven’t lived together. He had been afraid to ask anybody local to sign, again, because Norma’s brothers were so sneaky they might burn the person’s house down, or push their car over a cliff. He was surprised they hadn’t harassed him since he cut off their meal ticket.

He had thought of asking one of the deputy sheriffs to do it, but then he found out that his brother Josh was planning to stop and see him while on a business trip south with his wife. So he asked him to do it, and Josh agreed. The whole procedure took fifteen minutes. Norma didn't show up—he guessed she had seen so many television divorce cases that she thought it would be a big deal with several court appearances where she could drag him through the mud. Not so—he entered the court house married, and fifteen minutes later left, unmarried. The financial settlement made earlier still held.

Bev's reaction was positive, and she began to talk of living together permanently, but with all the hate stored up in him for Norma, and concern for his own kids, he just wasn't ready to get involved with anyone else's kids, or be tied down in any way. The physical relationship with Bev was excellent, although his mother raised hell about it all the time, calling her "that woman" in derogatory terms, but it was nice to have someone to confide in and discuss problems with.

Also, she and Josh and his wife had become friends, and the four of them had toured the countryside on a sightseeing trip that was a lot of fun. Bev had also been a lot of help to his sister, Esther, when her husband died—running errands, carting his sister around, organizing things. She was certainly a good person to have around —but not to be tied to.

His sister had not understood Josh's role in the divorce, and told others that her two brothers had gone to the courthouse and "swore out a pack of lies on Norma." No amount of persuasion could convince her of what really happened. But she had also accepted Bev, especially after all the help she was when Esther's husband died.

By now he and Bev had found time to travel some, and besides touring around the mountains on his motorcycle, since he had acquired a big one, they had also made a trip to Mexico—and were both impressed. They had also become regulars at blue grass festivals, and had even made a trip to see his other sister nine hundred miles away. All in all he felt that his life was looking up.

Then he started thinking about other things and other places in business. While at his brother-in-law's funeral, he casually mentioned to Josh that he was thinking of selling out, going to Mexico and trying writing full time. He even asked Josh if he would be interested. The upshot of this was that Josh was—the business would fit in well with what he was already doing, and the brothers even agreed on a price. A few days later Jed received a contract from Josh.

"I can't sign this," Jed said over the phone, "it says I can't be in this business for five years."

"That's right," said his brother, "it's a typical covenant-not-to-compete for a business transaction."

"Well, I can't agree to that," said Jed, "if I get down to Mexico and things don't work out, I'm coming back and starting up again."

"No you're not!" exclaimed Josh. "Not if I buy you out. That's all I'm buying, your customer list, your way of doing business, and any good will or contacts you've created along the way."

"What about all this equipment and supplies?"

"I don't need it," said Josh, "I'll either sell it where it sits, or throw it in the junk pile and take the write-off. It will cost more to move it than it's worth. Besides it's all outdated anyhow."

"Go to hell!" said Jed. "I don't care what you do, I'm going to Mexico for a year. Maybe I'll stay, maybe I won't. You can get into this business if you want to, I'm quitting as of the first of the month."

He never spoke to his brother again, and was especially chagrined when he felt like Josh was infringing on his territory a little later.

Someone else to hate!

Chapter 10, TOMMY

Jed's relationship with Bev hit an all-time low when he announced his plan to take a year off. She had been able to purchase a new mobile home, and get a new washer and dryer, plus a good used car from her income from his business, but she was heavily in debt.

"What am I going to do?" she asked him, as she saw the bottom dropping out from under her world.

"Go on welfare, I don't care," he said, sarcastically, "with all those kids you should be able to make out alright."

He didn't even say goodbye to her when he closed the place up and hit the road.

In Corpus Christi, in Mexico City, even in Acapulco, once he was away from close friends and business problems, one thought kept haunting him—were Craig and Tommy really his kids? Surely Norma meant they weren't his by means of his absence in raising them. But did she? There were all those years when they didn't have any children—and they were not practicing birth control. Was it his fault? Was he sterile?

It's probably too late to check that now, he thought.

But what about the soldier? When did that start? Was the soldier the first? Was he, Jed, the first? He remembered now that when they met she was wearing a bracelet with two hearts on it, and her initials on one heart and some others on the other. When he asked about it, she had told him it was from a brother of a friend of hers who was in the Army, and she had thrown the bracelet away when Jed bought her a new one on their second date. Was that the guy in the Army she was seeing after they split up?

And now he brooded about their honeymoon. She had said very emphatically that she was a virgin, but there was no physical evidence of it, based on what he had heard and read. Of course, he heard, it was sometimes like that, and it didn't seem to bother her, so it didn't bother him at the time. But now that he was alone and brooding, he wasn't sure.

Also, why wouldn't she ever go back up to her high school reunions? Was there someone there that might embarrass her? He had never been very jealous, figuring now that he had her, what did it matter who might admire her. But he didn't have her anymore—and after her remarks about the kids, it did matter.

After months of stewing about this and letting it upset his self-imposed exile, or sabbatical, whichever it was, he came to a conclusion. It might be too late to check his sterility, but it certainly wasn't too late to check on whether or not he was the father of the two boys. Blood tests would do the trick. He would start with the younger one—he wouldn't know what was going on anyway, and if there were no match, he would also check the older one.

With that decision made, he headed back for his home in the mountains.

When he told Norma of his suspicions, she was furious.

"Of course they're yours," she said, through tears streaming down her face, "I was never with any man before you! I don't know why we didn't have kids before. Maybe you ought to have yourself checked. Don't do this to Tommy. He's plenty big enough to know what is going on!"

"The appointments are already made," he growled, "I've got to know."

After a frightened thirteen year old had his blood tested, and it turned out to be exactly like that of the man he had always thought to be his father—there was someone else in the hating business. Even though Jed didn't pursue it further, and sometimes he would use his oldest son in his business, Tommy would never come anywhere near him again.

"It's still not conclusive," Jed told himself, "the other guy might have the same type of blood as me."

He still couldn't bring himself to get a sterility test—he wouldn't admit to being afraid of what he might find. It was easier to blame someone else, and go on hating.

A few days later he opened up his office again, and went to see Bev.

"I'm not coming back to you," she told him at the door. "I heard what you did to Tommy, and I don't want somebody that cold, heartless and cruel in my life, under any circumstances. Please don't bother me again."

And after all I did for her, Jed thought to himself. *I'll show her. I'll show them all that I am special. I'll put all those so-called friends, plus my idiot relatives, and especially my avaricious brother, in their places. I sure as hell don't need any of them, or their friendship. And, fortunately I am in a business I can run by myself. To hell with everybody!*

Epilogue, THE AWFUL TRUTH

As he topped Wallins Ridge Jed pulled off the highway to look back over the valley from which he had come. As the full moon rose behind him, he realized that he had spent the entire day driving and reminiscing through old haunts and old memories tracing his entire life in the process.

"I guess it wasn't so bad after all," he told himself. "No worse than lots of other people. At least I'll have a chance to see Mom one more time, and I'll make it up to my son, if it's the last thing I ever do. I'll get to know his kids, and treat them like the grandchildren they are. Of course, a reconciliation with my brother might be another problem, since he tried and I didn't. But, here I am past the half century mark and on the downhill slide. Maybe I'm the one to change."

Pulling into the parking area at Burr Oak, he couldn't help but think that his mother had never had a home since selling the place on the Knob—and his own need for money had triggered that. Also, as much as she had griped about disliking living "on this knob," as she put it, because it was too far from her church friends, and as much as she had hated and constantly condemned his father, Della had said that in recent years she had more and more referred to those years as the best of her life.

Now here she was, finishing out her life in a senior citizens' apartment complex, to which, according to Della, she had been sent back home by the doctors, who said could do no more for her.

Entering the apartment, he was met by Della and his cousin Herman, who had been visiting with his mother.

When he greeted them, a voice called him, fairly strong for a dying woman, from the single bedroom.

"Is that Jed, my baby?"

As all three entered the room, she ordered, in no uncertain terms, the first two to leave the room.

"I'd really like you to leave the apartment, I have to talk to Jed!"

"I guess I have a lot to say to you," Jed started, as he heard the door close behind the others.

"No, you listen to me," she said, in the same old demanding voice he had grown accustomed to in his childhood.

"But, Mom," he started again.

"Now, shut up and listen," she began. "I have to clear something up between me and the Lord before I die, and since you are part of it, I'll have to tell it to you. I can't go to meet my maker with this on my conscience."

"But why me?" he asked. "I haven't even seen you for years."

"Because you're my problem. Claude Burton Allen is not your daddy!"

"What?" he asked in consternation, a sudden fear engulfing him, so that he had to drop limply into his chair.

Was this lie her final jab at him? An attempt to destroy him totally? Apparently the hate was mutual.

"Didn't you ever wonder why you didn't look like any of the other kids? Or why your personality or intelligence level was not similar to theirs?

"Of course not," she went on, "but I'm going to tell you

about it, to ease my own conscience.

"When we moved to Briar Ridge, there I was stuck with three kids and a husband who coon-hunted every night. When he was home all he wanted was for me to read to him, since he couldn't read—old western books, anything. We never went anywhere or did anything. Never saw anybody, or had company.

"Some of the women in the camp started going to a church in town where they said they had a new preacher, a truly man of God. One night when Burt was hunting coons, they talked me into going with them—and I got saved.

"Preacher Williams baptized me in the creek, and I knew I had found the true way—my life became a religious one. I tried and tried to get Burt to go, but we quarreled about it more and more.

"I went to church every Wednesday and Saturday night, and Sunday morning and Sunday night. I could always get the neighbor's teen-age daughter to stay with the other kids.

"Burt always came to get me, though, because he knew how afraid I was of the dark.

"Then one night, before I left, we had our biggest quarrel. He throwed off on Brother Williams, that he was not a man of God, or anything else. He said some awful things to me, and told me I couldn't go to that church again. I showed him—I went anyway!

"When I came out after church, I didn't see him anywhere. Some of the other ladies said I could walk home with them, but I told them I would wait for Burt, since I didn't want him mad. Pretty soon they were all gone, and I was alone on the church steps. That's when Preacher Williams came out.

"When he found out my plight, he offered to walk me home. I was afraid at first, afraid of what Burt might do if he came and saw us. But I was even more afraid of being alone in the dark.

"On the way Brother Williams kept telling me how great it would be to follow his true calling by taking a godly woman like me and going throughout the world to preach the gospel. I got carried away, comparing the thought of that with my present life.

"As we approached Dead Man Bridge, a car was coming, so he suggested we walk down on the grassy bank under the bridge to avoid being seen together. There he kept talking about what a truly godly couple we were, with a message for the world! You can imagine what happened next—and Preacher Williams is your father!"

By now Jed was practically in a trance, with those last words still ringing in his ears.

"I know what you are thinking," she said, "but he's been dead for years. I hope he got right with the Lord before he went.

"As for me, after realizing what we had done, I went to see him the next day, only to find that he had packed his belongings and left the country—figuring, and rightly so, that if Burt found out he would kill him, and probably me, too."

By now Jed was like a wild man, seething with anger, but no way to let it out. When he raced past Della and Herman in the entryway to the building they noticed the blackness of his visage as he looked straight ahead, seeing nothing.

Two hours later and he was sitting on one of the remaining bridge abutments of what used to be Dead Man Bridge, staring at the grassy bank of the creek.

Hours later and he was hiking the trail above Briar Ridge, where he was born, and heading on around Big Black Mountain. From the ledge where the trail passed below the Window Rock, he stood for an interminably long time looking out over the lower ridges and valleys far to the south and east.

Going back to his car, he headed down through the Gap of the Mountain and out of these mountains forever. As he approached the head Rock, the bright moonlight shining on the face made him stop. It was as if he were drawn to it. Climbing up the rock-strewn hillside to the railroad bed that ran through and under the Rock, he paused to scan the precipitous side of the Rock itself.

Thinking how he had never been able to do anything he set out to do, he turned to the Rock. Nobody he knew had ever climbed it, and he just simply didn't try to scale any heights at all.

Sinking one hand in a crevice, he pulled himself up a couple of feet. That was easy, he thought. He did it again, and again. There were places where he was literally hanging on by his fingernails, but he kept going. At one place he had to crawl in a vertical crack and, bracing his back against one side, climb with his feet against the other. On he went, for hours on end, never looking down.

Suddenly he realized, as the sun climbed over Wallins Ridge in the distance, that he was almost to the last crack in the Rock—a good two hundred feet from where he started, and he had done it with no light except the moon!

Exultantly, he shouted out loud, "I did it. I did something no one else can do, not even my brother!"

As he reached for the top of the rock in the bright morning sunlight, he heard the rattles too late.

Throwing up both hands to shield his face from the deadly strike of the sunning snake, he lost his footing in the crack, and caroming off the next projection, sailed head first toward the brush-covered rocks, two hundred feet below.

And he was smiling all the way!

THE END

PREFACE, Bud

His whole family and friends around Woodway call him "Bud," and he would tell you right up front that he is a sterile engineer. No, he's not an engineer that works on sterile projects. His college degree says he's a mechanical engineer—and he has held several important satisfying positions in business and industry related to it. But he is also sterile. And no, he is not a super clean man. It means he cannot father children, can't get anybody pregnant. That goes back to when he was about ten years old, and got mumps. The disease "fell on him," as the old folks say. It settled in his testicles, which swelled up to the size of baseballs, and made him very uncomfortable for a couple of weeks. After he recuperated, he heard the doctor telling his dad that he would never be able to make him a grandfather. Bud didn't understand that at first, but it slowly sank into his ten-year-old mind, as he learned a little more about where, and how, babies come from. But over time it became both a blessing and a curse, starting with his first visit to "The Crossroads Store" when he met his little girl friend Carmen. He liked girls. He always had. Still does. He could load them up with "baby juice," but there was nothing live in it. Some could get what they wanted from him, some could not. It's a major part of the story of his life. When he met a girl that he would like to spend the rest of his life with, all they wanted was a roll in the hay occasionally, with no fear of an unwanted pregnancy. But quite often, when he met some hottie that all he wanted was some casual sex, they started talking about a lifetime commitment—in an adoptive mode, no less. So he stayed single. But his life was not all about girls. He said he's not a special person, nothing extraordinary about him. He was more of an ordinary guy to whom extraordinary things happen. Besides girls, this included secondary school, college, the military, sports, hobbies, and other relationships. That's why he decided to get someone to try and write his story. So here goes. Maybe they'll make a movie of it.

CHAPTER ONE, Carmen

This particular day was the day Carmen and Bud became intimate. Oh, they had been somewhat intimate since they were eight years old, but now they were almost twelve. When he was eight, his folks left him at his grandparents' home in the country near Jonesville, the county seat, for a few weeks in the summer. Although he was learning to do many farm chores, as the summer wore on, Bud became restless because of his boredom—no other kids to play with. Discerning his problem, his grandparents gave him some money and suggested he walk up to the local crossroads general store and get himself some candy.

Hiking along the tree-lined dusty dirt road, Bud was enjoying feeling his bare feet first in the hot summer sand of the road, then in the cooler areas as he walked in the shade of trees. Eventually he saw a somewhat white building on which were painted the fading words, "Crossroads Store, General Merchandise." Although the store was on a paved road, the one leading from his grandparents' farm to the store was dirt—or mostly sand. In front of the store was a hand activated gasoline pump. Climbing the steps which led to a porch running clear across the front of the building, Bud spotted a skinny girl about his age, wearing a white summer sun dress, held up on her small bare shoulders by thin spaghetti straps. She was bare footed, like Bud, and sitting on a wicker chair reading a book. She had long dark hair, and when she looked up at him, he discovered bright brown curiously staring eyes.

"Hi, I'm Carmen," she said. "Who're you?"

Somewhat taken aback by her open forward manner, he stammered, "I'm Bud. I'm staying with my grandpa down the road. I came up here to buy some candy."

"We have a lot of it," she said. "My parents run the store. C'mon, I'll help you pick out some candy."

Following her into the store, Bud thought they could immediately become friends. She might be more fun than his grandpa and grandma.

After they obtained the candy, she said, "Want to see my playhouse?"

He thought he had no choice but to say yes. So he followed her around in back of the store. The store was sitting on the side of a hill that sloped away to the rear, so that the receiving dock was about four feet off the ground. Under this platform, Carmen's father had built her a playhouse—complete with walls, a door, and carpeting on the dirt floor. It contained a table, two chairs, and shelves for her dolls. A great place to play. Bud even played with her dolls, the ones that were supposed to be boys.

After they had played for a while, Carmen surprised him by saying, "Bud, want to see my butt?"

"Well, yeah," he said.

He knew that you were not supposed to see anybody's "hockey butt," in back, or "pee butt," in front, as his folks called them, or let anybody see yours. That's why people wore clothes. He didn't know why, but somehow it was somewhat naughty to see or be seen in those areas. But here was a little girl who wanted to break that rule.

So she bent over, with her back to him, pulled her dress up, and yanked her flimsy pink panties down, sticking her little bare rear butt out towards him. Nothing unusual there. It looked a lot like his.

"Now show me yours," she said.

So he complied. Neither of them had learned to appreciate looking at each others front pee butts. What boys' and girls' front parts were used for, besides peeing, was not yet known to them.

a few more. They all giggled, and none complained or reported him to the teacher. Then as the years went by, and he advanced from grade to grade, he ventured farther afield. One day he happened to come by a drinking fountain just as one of the girls in his class bent over to get a swig of water. Her short skirt slid up high enough to reveal her scanty pink underwear. Bud couldn't resist it. Not even wondering what his punishment might be if he got caught, he patted her gently on one side of her almost-exposed bottom. When she did not respond, he patted her on the other side. She turned and smiled, a big satisfied smile. Then when he bent over to get a drink, she shoved her hand up between his legs into his crotch, and squeezed his testicles and penis profusely.

When he turned around, she spread her hands openly, and said, "Just takin' my turn."

Now he had a new pursuit. Bud wondered if any of the other boys went around patting the girls on their bottoms—or getting their appendages squeezed. He had not seen any of boys doing it, so he never mentioned it to any of them.

He did not return to his grandparents farm that summer, because that was when he got the mumps.

Then when he arrived back at his grandparents for a visit the year he and Carmen both turned almost twelve, things changed. Carmen was again on the porch of the store, reading a book. When he greeted her, she produced a softball, and wanted to play catch out behind the store. She was wearing shorts and a shirt, instead of her usual flimsy dress. They were very reservedly tossing the ball back and forth, when he threw her one she missed. It went into a small clump of cedar trees, and she could not find it. So Bud walked over to help. She was sitting on a rock, with her shirt unbuttoned, revealing a small pink brassiere. He found the ball, and they went on with their game. He felt sorry for her, because she could not keep her shirt buttoned. The next one she missed, and he had to go help find it. Again her blouse was unbuttoned. Bud decided to be funny.

Next thing he knew she was stroking his now-erect penis with both hands. Then she lay back down on the soft grassy ground, spreading her legs slightly invitingly. Bud did not know exactly how to do this, but he slid up on top of her, while she reached down with her hands and guided things together. He started penetration into her with his penis, but felt a slight obstruction. He was afraid he might hurt her, if his penis would not go in. But she grabbed both his butt cheeks and pulled slightly, and suddenly he and Carmen were jammed together, as she uttered a slight cry of pain, or was it ecstasy? His hard penis was all the way in her juicy opening. They both had orgasms almost immediately. Like all young boys, he had treated himself occasionally, but he had never dreamed that anything could bring him this much pleasure. Her own ecstasy was undeniable.

When he started to withdraw, she grabbed his cheeks again, whispering, "Not yet, not ever!"

Soon they did it again—and again. When they finally separated, exhausted, he realized they were both bloody messes.

"We'll sneak in the house and clean up," she said. "My folks will be at the store for a long time yet."

This became their pattern then, for the rest of his summer visit. He would meet her at the store, then they would do it multiple times in her playhouse, which had no dolls anymore, the grove, one of the bedrooms in her parents house next door to the store, the living room couch or floor, or many other places. They also even learned how to stand up and do it quickly if time was of the essence.

Just a few days before Bud had to return to his folks at Woodway and school at Elk Knob, he went to see her, and was directed to her under-store playhouse. She was waiting for him, but had another girl their age in tow.

"This is my cousin, Gretchen," she said. "She's visiting for a few days. Let's all do the massaging."

Carmen pulled a bottle of the sunburn lotion off a shelf, and took off the cap. So far this summer they had not used it, but he guessed that it would be an innocuous activity for the three of them. But no, Carmen immediately took off all her clothes, and Gretchen smilingly did the same. Her cousin had a little more in the breasts and butt than Carmen, but both girls were desirably great looking. So he removed his clothing too. Soon they were rubbing each other all over, but the girls said no lotion in their crotches. From the way the two girls rubbed each other, he suspected they had done this before. After all, they surely slept together, and so…

Gretchen seemed particularly interested in stroking Bud's erection. He suspected she had never seen a boy with a hard on before. She lay back on the carpet, spreading her legs, and Carmen motioned for him to do her cousin first. He didn't need much encouraging. Within two minutes they had both come, and he hated to stop. But he did. Then Carmen started rubbing his penis, until he was ready to explode again. And he did, inside her. They repeated their turnabout pattern for the rest of the day, until Bud was completely fagged out. But the next day they did it again, and every day, until he had to return home for school. Bud began the think of the Crossroads Store as his own section of paradise—and he believed that Carmen felt the same way.

CHAPTER TWO, Grade School

Bud did not know how they knew, but it seems like everyone he met at Elk Knob School knew about his affliction. The boys might mention it, but the girls just looked at him kind of funny. Or was it his sensitive imagination, he wondered. He went on as if nothing had happened when he was ten, or during the past summer. His activities, with Carmen, and her cousin too, were too far-fetched to be believable. Sometimes he wondered if he had dreamed the whole series of events.

Then in seventh grade he met Margret. Suddenly she was in his class, and the teacher was introducing this new girl. When Bud turned to look at her, she swiveled towards him in her seat, spreading her legs, to reveal bloody spots in her panties to him.

Well, she is growing up, at least, like Carmen, he thought.

Her parents had moved to the Woodway area a few weeks after school started. Margret had joined the girls' basketball team at the school immediately. Bud thought she was pretty good. They played on an outdoor court, and wore typical basketball uniforms—shorts and tops. He liked looking at all the female players' attributes, but Margret seemed special—nice figure, long legs, long blond hair, blue eyes. One day during lunch hour, she approached him as he sat on one of the school porch banisters.

"They tell me you know where that creek comes from," she said, pointing to the stream that flowed past the school.

Of course he did, he had explored the area around it many times.

"Will you take me there?" she asked.

"It would have to be on the weekend," he said. "There is not enough time during a school day."

So she agreed to meet him the very next Saturday. She showed up in shorts and a white top, and Bud had dressed similarly. They set out. The creek flowed out of a spring in a glen surrounded by trees, a half mile or so above the school. Soon they were getting a cold drink from the spring, and sitting on some rocks getting cool by the opening. Then taking off their shoes and socks, he held Margret's hand, leading her a short distance into the creek. When the creek got too deep, they turned around and started back out. At this juncture, Margret slipped on the wet rocks, and fell, sitting in the cold water well above her waist. She laughingly reached up and pulled Bud down in the creek with her. She stood up, and surprised him by putting her arms around his neck, and kissing him full on the lips. In all the years he had played with Carmen, and her cousin—and even when he had been patting his fellow students on the butt, no one had ever hugged or kissed him. Now Margret was doing it over and over again, in the coolness of the creek. Bud did nothing to discourage her. When he led her back up onto the lush grass of the glen, she yanked off her wet top and shorts, revealing that she had nothing under them except the naturally blond hair in her crotch. She spread the clothing by her on the grass to dry, and motioned for Bud to do the same, which he obligingly did. Then she plopped down on the lush green creek bank in a supine position. Pulling him down on top of her, she began kissing him again.

"Is it true what I hear about you?" she asked.

"I don't know. What have you heard?"

"That no girl has anything to worry about, when she is with you," she said.

"I would never hurt anybody, if that is what you mean."

"It's not what I mean, and you know that."

With that, she pulled him closer. Bud knew exactly what to do, although he had not done it since Carmen. Wrapped in each others arms, kissing constantly, his insertion was simple, because of his stiffness and her juiciness. Their orgasms ran repeatedly, until they were worn out. Bud rolled over, and they continued to lie in each others arms. He suspected that Margret, though very young, had done this before. That didn't bother him at all. He was happy to be with her.

"We are now a couple going steady," she then said, demandingly. "So you must not do this with anyone but me. I'm your girlfriend."

Bud did not answer. He kept thinking of Carmen. He liked Margret, but preferred being with Carmen. So he just chuckled.

"Don't you see it that way, too?" she asked.

"I'm afraid not," he replied. "We are too young to make that kind of commitment."

"Then you can't have me anymore," she said sternly.

So what, he thought. *This whole thing was her idea. She is the one that set it up.*

And later he suspected that she had confided her disappointment to her girlfriends, because for the rest of that school year, and the following eighth grade year, Bud had many similar experiences with several girls—usually it was the first time of such an event for most of them. But very few wanted to do it again, as Carmen had. Although they seemed to enjoy it immensely, he suspected they had second thoughts—or somehow felt guilty. He had heard of such things, but never felt that way himself. Whenever he thought of it at all, he just accepted the fact that it was a normal human desire and activity. He understood that the basic need was to procreate, but since he could not, he just enjoyed the pleasurable side of it. Bud never discussed his exploits with anyone—boys or girls.

He almost hated to have to leave the country school the following year and go into Pennington, the nearby town, to high school—but most of the girls he knew attended there, too.

CHAPTER THREE, High School

The last summer before high school, Bud went back to the country to visit his grandparents, and help with their chores as much as he could. When he hiked up to the store on his second day there, Carmen was expecting him. When she met him on the porch of the store, he broke their usual beginning routine by putting his arms around her and kissing her soundly on the lips. She responded accordingly. Holding hands, they walked back to the clump of cedars where they had first become intimate.

After he kissed her again, he said, "I want to tell you right up front, I have missed you. You must know I think the world of you."

Looking at him out of the corners of her lovely sparkling brown eyes, she said, "What would you think of a girl who could not tell a boy she loved him?"

"If this were the case," he said, "I'd think she was wonderful, no matter if she ever told him, because I love her."

"You know I do love you," she said. "I have ever since we first met."

"I do know, Carmen," he said. "You would not have done what you did with me unless you loved me."

"About that," she said, "my Mom said only married people should do that. Did we do something wrong?"

"Married people do it for both pleasure and to make babies," Bud said, guardedly. "Since I cannot make babies, I could only do it for pleasure. And I don't think that was wrong. And we both enjoyed it."

"Yes, immensely," she said. "That's why I brought Gretchen along that day. I wanted her to have what I had, but then I got jealous of the way you enjoyed her."

"We were awful young," Bud said. "Neither of us really knew what we were doing."

"Well, I don't want to do it anymore, until we get it all figured out."

"Fine by me," he said, holding Carmen close, and kissing her passionately.

Soon they were entwined in each other, naked on the lush grass of the glade.

"So much for that commitment," said Carmen afterwards. "I guess we just can't help it."

So this visit of Bud's to his grandparents became just like all the others, only this time he hated leaving Carmen's love behind to return to his home.

As he entered high school, he was constantly besieged by girls who wanted to be alone with him. Thinking of his love for Carmen, he avoided such contacts as much as possible—especially since some of them were totally undesirable girls, demanding, flamboyant, braggarts, sometimes absolute "uggos!" He did not want to be connected with them.

To get to school Bud normally walked from his home to the country grade school building at Elk Knob, where he boarded a school bus for Pennington. The school janitor was still in grade school, but was old enough to have graduated from high school many years before. He just kept attending the school because of his job there. He usually had a group of boys enhanced with his tales before school took up in the morning down in the basement of the school building. Not really a basement, just a big hole in the ground with no walls. But it contained the coal-fired furnace and water boiler, since the six rooms and auditorium of the school were heated by steam radiators. This had not changed for Bud after starting high school. He still liked to visit with the janitor, affectionately known as "Hoot" by the other boys—while waiting for the bus. Bud especially enjoyed the discussions of sex by all the members of the group—most of whom knew very little about it, especially less than he knew. He offered no information or corrections to their errors. He did notice that Hoot seemed to be pretty well-informed.

One day he almost laughed out loud when a swaggering eighth-grader remarked that girls do not like sex, they just do it to pay for their dates. Then another made him chuckle when he said that all girls "shoot off" like a boy when they come, and it will get all over you. Also, most of the boys were always looking for ways to see more of a girl than normal. One of them confessed to the group that he had mounted a mirror down low on the front wheel fork of his bicycle, so that when he let a girl ride on the bars between his legs, he could look down into the mirror and see up under her dress. Another said that girls don't like to have boys look at them. Even though they might remove enough clothing for you to get to them, they do not want you to see them naked. Bud laughed to himself.

Bud had to smile at all these ruses, when he knew exactly how to see everything about a girl that he wanted to—as well as how to touch them all the way.

The only advice that Bud heard from Hoot that was true was that if initially you touched a girl inappropriately, they feel violated, but if you can arrange for them to touch you, all the stops are out. Bud thought all boys knew that, but Hoot said no they don't, and that is how they get in trouble.

Then one morning one of the boys was discussing the relationship between his older brother and Hoot's cousin, Hazel, who lived up in a hollow of the mountain.

"I don't know if they are doing it," said Hoot. "Probably are. But he would have found a lot more excitement over in the next holler with Inez, as I have—as well as two of my brothers. She is always a sure thing."

Gee, how have I missed her? thought Bud, laughing to himself.

As time went on Bud was to learn that Hoot was getting it on regularly with Bud's neighbor Virginia, Bud's friend Floyd and his neighbor Georgia weren't missing out on anything, and neither were his friends Brad and Evelyn.

One morning when he approached the Elk Knob grade school, Bud saw smoke coming from the holes around the foundation leading to the furnace room. Racing through the door to the room, he found that the furnace had exploded, and Hoot was lying unconscious on the dirt floor. Bud grabbed him and dragged him out through the doorway. Then seeing flames lapping at the floors of the school, he ran through the building yelling for everyone to get out. As all the children ran away from the structure, Bud checked all the rooms and the auditorium for stragglers. Finding none, he raced for the doorway, and herded all the kids away from the building. By the time a fire truck arrived, the school building had burned to the ground.

Bud was hailed as a hero, but just shrugged it off. He had just done what had to be done.

He was enjoying high school, especially all the math classes. And he realized he had not really understood English until he started taking a course in Latin. There were still brief interludes with girls, which he accepted as a matter of course. Nothing special—no surprises, until...

Janet had been in many of his classes. She had been friendly, but he did not know her very well. Someone had told him that she came from one of the better families in town. She dressed well for a high school student, her dishwater blond hair was always fixed neatly, and her hazel eyes lit up often in a bright smile. She kept her legs smooth shaven, and her nails neatly trimmed and polished. One day she approached him outside the school building on the walk during their lunch hour.

"Do you know where the swirl hole is in the river?" she asked.

"Yes," he said. "It's down behind the Odd Fellows Tabernacle near Woodway. I have fished there many times."

"Will you take me there?"

"Sure. Do you want to go fishing? It's not a bad place to swim, either."

"I want to camp there all night," she said. "Me and my friend, Ruby, and her boyfriend. And of course, you, if you are game."

Then it came out that Ruby and Jim wanted to spend the night somewhere together—something they had not done so far—so they had decided that each girl would tell her parents that she was spending the night at the others' house. Jim and Ruby were a couple, at least around school—but Bud did not know how close they were. Obviously Janet just wanted to be with Bud. Bud was game, so the four teenagers met at the designated place on the river at sundown. Bud had borrowed a flat-bottomed skiff from a friend, and just to play it safe, in case it rained, turned it upside down over a grassy spot on the river bank, with the bow propped up on a large driftwood log. He and Janet placed their blankets under it, while Jim and Ruby decided to rough it, spreading their blankest on a sandbar.

As soon as it got dark, the girls announced it was time to go skinny dipping, but insisted the boys stay away from them. Of course, as soon as the now nude girls entered the water, Bud yanked off his clothes and swam over to Janet. Soon they were dried off and under the upturned boat.

Then Bud heard Ruby exclaim, from their blankets, "What do you mean, you don't have any? You knew what the results of this was going to be, didn't you?"

Then Jim said, "I bet Bud don't have any, either."

"Bud don't need any," said Ruby. "Everybody knows that."

Their voices then became muffled, as Bud and Janet went on doing what they had come there for, until he heard Jim stalking away, through the woods along the shore. After a long time, while Bud and Janet were lying side by side, in each others arms, Ruby slid under the boat with them.

"I hope you don't mind, Janet," she said, "but I don't want to see this become a futile camping trip."

Just as Janet moved to one side to make room for her girlfriend, Jim came back, and not seeing Ruby anywhere, started calling for her. She was hesitant to answer him, until he said he had what they needed. Then she crawled out from under the boat, and joined Jim on their blankets. Bud could see in the moonlight that they were immediately nude and wrapped in each others arms.

"Oh, shucky darns, Bud," Janet said, "An opportunity missed for you to get a double."

"I wouldn't have been much good, Babe," he said. "You already wore me out."

"Oh, no, I was hoping for much more!"

"All I can do is try," Bud said, knowing full well that he and Janet could and would go on doing this all night.

Bud thought this was to be a one-shot deal, like so many other girls—but Janet fooled him. He was surprised, in succeeding days, at how often she wanted to do this again—under much more comfortable circumstances. On a day when he stopped by her house, per her invitation, he discovered no one was home. When he rang the doorbell, he heard her voice calling him to come on in. Then after she identified it was him, she loudly told him she was in the bathroom, to come on back.

As he entered the bathroom, he was pleasantly surprised to see a nude Janet sitting in the bathtub.

"Here you go, Bud," she said, handing him a wash cloth, "wash my back."

Soon Bud was washing more than her back, and soon after that they were wrapped in each others arms on her bed.

Such occasions manifested themselves often, and Bud did not try to fight her off, just accepted it as a way of life, and part of his school experiences.

Then for his junior year English class he was surprised to have a beautiful new teacher. Her name was Miss Ervin. She was fresh out of college—probably twenty or twenty-one, Bud guessed. Built like the proverbial brick outhouse, well-dressed, long legs, lovely natural red hair, blue eyes—dressed much like the high school girls, skirts and blouses or sweaters and bobby socks. What if one of her eyes did turn inward towards her nose? To Bud her being cross-eyed was not detrimental at all. She liked to teach sitting on her desk in the center at the front of her room. Bud liked to sit smack dab in the middle, facing her, where he could look at her beautiful face and hair, her smooth-shaven legs and sometimes pink panties, or sometimes butt cheeks. He made up his mind to try to get closer to her, maybe by asking her out—maybe next year, when he was a senior. But then he knew of a sophomore boy who dated a grade school teacher. Of course the soph was older than Bud, and should have graduated long ago. Still Miss Ervin obviously had no boyfriend—most guys her age were in the military. So one afternoon after school when she had stayed late, he found a way to walk home with her, just the two of them, trying to get to know her better.

She had a room in the only hotel in the town of Pennington, and he suspected she lived very frugally. She surprised Bud by inviting him in. Looking around her room he spotted a small hotplate, on which she could fix minimal meals—but Bud guessed that she ate most of her meals out, in one of the three restaurants in town.

As his six-foot frame towered over her in her small room, Miss Ervin turned, put her arms around him, tilted her head back, pulled his face down close to hers, and kissed him. Shocked, he really believed she was just relieving the tensions of an all-girls college with no one to date. But no, she wanted more.

Pulling away from him, as she entered the nearby bathroom, over her shoulder she said, "I'll be right back."

Confused, Bud sat on the edge of her bed and waited. Perhaps she just had to pee, or something more serious. He still waited. Soon Miss Ervin came strutting invitingly out of the bathroom, completely nude! And all her hair was the same color, that delicious red. Her collar and cuffs matched, he realized. Bud's eyes hungrily took in all of her. He was delighted and immediately eager!

"Now you," she said. "Use the bathroom."

"Miss Ervin," he started to say.

"It's Rebecca, when we are like this," she said, waving him towards the bathroom door.

Soon Bud came back out of the bathroom, clean and relieved, but now dressed just like her. That is to say, no clothing at all. He found her lying on the bed with her legs spread.

"I do not expect you to have rubbers," she whispered, "but I have some."

"Not needed. I'm sterile," he said.

She seemed delighted when he told her about the mumps.

“Great,” she said. I’ve been looking for a man like you. But go slow. It’s been a long time. Let’s just kiss and touch a bit at first.”

So, he thought, *she has done this before. And she knows what to do.*

And did she ever! Bud was in for the ride of his life. No more fumbling around with first-time school girls. Soon their passionate kissing, caressing and stroking accomplished its purpose, and both of them were ready. Rebecca had been there and done that—perhaps many times. And she did it many times now. She started by pulling her knees almost up to her chin, then spreading them, with her crotch lifted just right for insertion. Later she would lie flat on her back, with her legs spread, then move them tight against him, as he moved up and down. Then he realized that the natural pulsation that he had been experiencing could be caused deliberately by his own efforts. She seemed delighted by this action. She liked also to lie on her side, with him on his side, facing each other—while still plugged in together. Then she arose to a sitting position on him, sliding down over his hardened penis, and moving up and down, as he continued pulsating.

“That’s new to me,” she whispered, “don’t stop.”

Bud counted at least eight orgasms for her, to three for him. Every time he started to withdraw, she would pull him in further, holding him tight by the buttocks. As a final gesture, she rolled over on her hands and knees, so he could enter her differently—a position of which he was heretofore unaware. But the sensation was marvelous.

When they finally finished to the satisfaction of both of them, she smilingly headed for the bathroom again. This time coming out wearing an unfastened bathrobe. Bud had almost dozed off, but woke up when she reappeared. Rebecca came over to him, still smiling, when he sat up on the edge of the bed. Rebecca leaned in towards him, placing her nipples near his face, indicating she wanted them kissed. Doing so, as she writhed in ecstasy, he reached under her robe to squeeze her buttocks, and then to stroke that silky red hair again.

Backing off, she whispered, “Enough for now. More next time!”

So there would be a next time, he thought. *Not like the one-timer school girls.*

From that time on until the end of the school year, Rebecca and Bud made love at least once a week— and sometimes more, unless she had a period. When she left for the summer, Bud was glad to go back to Carmen. But he looked forward to the next school year and Miss Ervin. It was not to be. Miss Ervin did not return. Another teacher told him she got married to some G.I. and was teaching in Florida, where he was stationed.

Lucky G.I., thought Bud.

His own school year flew by. He looked forward to graduation, and planned to enlist in the Army as soon as he did. There were still a few school girls to deflower, plus a few, like Janet, that were already done and wanted a repeat experience. But after Rebecca, everybody else seemed amateurish.

CHAPTER FOUR, The Army

With his father’s permission Bud joined the Army immediately after graduation from high school. With a war on, he knew he would be drafted as soon as he turned eighteen anyway, so he might as well get his obligation for military service out of the way. He was looking forward to the experience. After his preliminary physical examination, and being given a date as to when he was to report for duty, he drove his dad’s car down to the Crossroads Store to visit Carmen. She greeted him with a series of warm kisses and hugs, and soon they were making love on the lush green grass in their favorite grove of trees.

"I probably won't be here when you come home on your first leave," she said, leaning back to absorb him in those beautiful brown eyes. "I'll be away in college."

"Maybe I can still work something out, so we can be together," he said.

"What do you plan to do after the war is over and your service time is up?"

"I don't know right now, probably go to college, if possible. I'd like to be some sort of engineer. Math and drafting were my favorite subjects in high school."

"And then you'll marry me?" she said, smiling and squeezing his hand.

"No, you do not want to be saddled with a man who cannot make you a mother."

"But I want you!" she exclaimed. "I want to go down life's road with you, no matter where it leads."

"You'll change your mind about that, as time goes on, Carmen. Every woman wants to be a mother. But I will come to see you, and be your close friend, until you find the right guy."

But it was not to be. He could never get a schedule where he could visit her. It looked like his military time might be long and lonesome. No time or opportunities for any girls during his basic training, and then he was off to North Africa on his first overseas assignment. No leaves for soldiers in that area, and the couple of weekend passes he had were boring—just a few strange drinks with other soldiers in a local tavern. Meantime, he had been promoted to Corporal, and was involved in keeping his own squad well-trained and ready, for whenever they had to do some shooting. Soon he was tired of the spasmodic war on the hot desert sands, and was pleased that his group was to be sent to Sicily in the Mediterranean.

It didn't take long for the heat and humidity of that island nation to get to him either, so when his outfit was transferred to England to prepare for what Bud thought was to be an upcoming invasion of Europe, he was pleased. He liked seeing green grass and trees, and the cool dampness didn't bother him at all. By the time the invasion did come, he was a Sergeant, with much more authority and responsibility.

CHAPTER FIVE, The Dairy Farm

Soon after arriving in England he was informed that idle G.I.s were to go and help local businesses whenever possible, since there was now an extreme shortage of British men. Bud thought anything would beat the endless boredom of continuous repetitive training, just to keep the men busy. So, studying the bulletin board, he volunteered for duty at a dairy farm, about four miles from where he was stationed. He thought his experiences with cattle on his grandparents' farm could be useful. Hiking out to the farm on his first day, not knowing what to expect, he was carrying a can of coffee and a change of clothes in his backpack.

As soon as he arrived, he was introduced to the manager—who turned out to be a nineteen year old girl named Cornelia. Very pretty, he thought, even in her knee-high rubber boots for the damp soil, and baggy work clothes. But she looked older than her nineteen years. Probably the wartime life she had been forced to live, he guessed. She wore no makeup that Bud could see. It seemed she was running the place with a minimum of very young boys—grade school level—and very old men—who should have been retired.

"Call me Corny," she said, very businesslike. "We'll spend this first day getting you acquainted with our operation."

Her hair was short and naturally blond, and her eyes were a deep blue, but seemed to be lifeless, as if her thoughts were always far away. Bud was to learn that Corny had a boyfriend in the British Navy, but his ship being assigned to the Australian area, had not been home for a long time—and probably would not be.

Very few things were different from his grandparents' farm, so he knew he fit right in. He enjoyed touring the milking and feeding barn, and especially the big green pasture field. By eight o'clock that evening, he was fairly well versed in what he would be doing. Corny offered him a cup of tea, which he accepted—not wanting to push her into making coffee, which he didn't think a Britisher would want to drink with him, anyway.

"It's very late for you to be hiking back to you Quonset hut," she said. "You could just sleep on my divan, if you like, and if no one would miss you."

"I'd like to stay. I'm tired, and I won't be missed. What about your crew?"

"They all live off the farm," she said. "I live here alone."

"I'll be happy to accept your hospitality," he said.

"Good," she said. "You can take a bath, after I do. We do not have a shower. Too bad you will have to wear the same clothing again."

Bud assured her that he had other clothing with him. Soon he was clean, and stretched out on the couch. Shortly Corny came in, wearing a loose bathrobe, and sat on the edge of his couch.

"It's good that you brought clean clothing," she said. "You know, all I do is work. I have no social life at all. Too bad you didn't bring some rubbers, or our sleeping arrangements might be a little cozier. I'm sure you have some in your belongings back at your quarters. All Americans do. It's been a long time for me, and probably just as long for you—unless you have been hitting the redlight district."

"No, I've never done that," Bud said. "And I do not carry rubbers. Don't have to."

Then he told her about his sterile condition. She seemed to just accept that, like she had all the fortunes of war. She led him into her bedroom, dropping the bathrobe to the floor. He was somewhat startled to see that she had not shaved her legs or her armpits. He recalled other service men refer to their British girlfriend acquaintances as "limey pigs." Maybe they all looked like Cornelia. But no, she was definitely not a pig—just grown careless, with no one to impress. Apparently she was right—she did nothing but work. Cornelia was slightly plump but solid. She had a very well-shaped butt and legs, and large breasts. Her nipples were a pretty pink, and almost as big as marbles. Soon they were sharing her bed, and Bud could tell that she had been missing this, by her eagerness to please—both him and herself. She was very well versed in the art of what they were doing.

That Navy boyfriend must have been a very active man, Bud thought.

In spite of their long day and tired conditions, they enjoyed each other immensely. Bud was beginning to look forward to his time on the dairy farm.

When he awoke the next morning Cornelia was still in the bathroom. When she came out, all the hair was gone from her legs and underarms.

"I'm trying to look a little neater for you," she said, smiling. "Thought you might like me better."

"I think I would like you, no matter what," he replied. "You are a beautiful woman—warm, sweet and wonderful."

And she was. But there was something about her that appealed to Bud even more than her appearance. He thought it might be her straightforward manner—almost businesslike about everything, even their bedroom relations. She had her feet planted firmly on the ground—knew just what she wanted, and how to get it.

Nothing frivolous about this girl, he thought.

Somehow he liked it—so different from other girls he had known.

But what about himself? Why would he appeal to so many women? Maybe it was just that he was available and safe. Still, when he looked in a mirror, he saw a tall clean-cut young man, with a big white-toothed smile topped by a well-trimmed mustache.

I'd like to think I would be appealing even if I was not sterile, he thought.

Over the next few weeks Bud settled into their routine and relationship, as if he had always done that. The open fresh air, the smell of the hay, brought him some memories of home. He even acquired a bicycle to get back and forth to the dairy farm more easily. He found himself putting the possibility of joining an invading military force far back in his mind. But all this was to change before the war caught up with him again.

It started when his commanding officer called him into his office one morning. He was told that he was being assigned as a helper at a ship building company on the coast.

"It's no further than you are going now," said the officer, "so you can still ride your bicycle down there."

"When do I start?" Bud asked, hoping he would be able to say goodbye to Cornelia first.

"Today," said the man. "This is more important than what you are doing, because it directly affects what we are all planning for the war effort. They have a shortage of critical technicians, and your experience as a draftsman and knowledge of math will fit right in."

So Bud never saw Corny again.

CHAPTER SIX, The Shipyard

Riding his bike down to the shipyard a little later, Bud couldn't help but notice the congested conditions of the area—buildings and boats, or parts of boats, everywhere. Arriving at the building to which he had been directed, he was shown to a drawing board and desk. There were several other men, and a few women, at similar work stations in a large office-type work bay. Most of the men looked old, but most of the women looked young. One young woman with a friendly manner approached him immediately. Bud noticed that she was about six inches shorter than him, and had short dark hair and blue eyes. Her short tan skirt and white blouse revealed a voluptuous figure.

"I'm Nora, and I'm your group leader," she said. "Our job is to record on drawings the changes or improvements made on boats, after the fact. That way, all future boats will include them."

Bud thanked her, and set about his first assigned task. He had to go examine a boat, measure and sketch the improvements, then go back to his drawing board and record the changes. The work was tedious and boring, and he was using very little of his math and drawing knowledge.

A couple of days later, one of the women came to a pencil sharpener mounted on a post near Bud. When she finished her task, and turned away, she dropped a pencil. One of the old men sitting near her reached down and retrieved the pencil, but instead of returning it to her, he ran his hand up the girl's bare leg. When his hand got about halfway up her thigh, she squealed and jerked away. Bud was to learn that this occurred quite often—with other girls and other men. Maybe it was a game they played—perhaps the pencil-dropping was planned. Over time he thought it might be a way to relieve the boredom, so one day somebody dropped a pencil near him, and he went through the same motions. Running his hand up to the point of no return, halfway up her thigh, she did not move. Soon his hand met some flimsy panties. Twisting his head up, he spotted the typical tan skirt of Nora. Suddenly he realized that he had never seen any of the men do this to her—or she had simply never dropped a pencil. After all, she was the boss.

Leaning her face down close to his ear, she whispered, "What are you going to do now?"

Taking the bull by the horns, Bud handed her the pencil and boldly whispered back, "I know what I'd like to do, and soon."

"Then walk me home tonight. It's not very far," she said.

Entering her home with her later, Bud deliberately held her hand tightly, to signify his intentions. She pointed out that this was her parents' home, but that she had her own apartment upstairs. Shedding his coat, as she shed hers, as they entered her apartment, he then spun her around to face him, and kissed her soundly on the mouth.

Leaning back, she said, “No messing around in advance. I like that. My folks won’t be home for a while. Let’s get in bed.”

Soon they were on her bed, making up for lost time. Nora did not even mention rubbers to him. Maybe she knew something he didn’t. He decided to keep silent about his sterility, unless Nora brought it up. Later, as they lay exhausted on the bed, Bud panicked when he thought he heard a door open.

“That would be my parents,” Nora said. “Don’t worry. They won’t come up here.”

Getting dressed, Bud and Nora headed down the stairs.

Introducing her folks, she pointed out to a shocked Bud that they owned the shipyard. No wonder that she was the boss of the design unit. Both parents seemed delighted when Nora introduced him as her new boyfriend. Over time he was to find out why.

Over the next few weeks Bud’s design job became more interesting, and so did Nora. They were together after work almost every night, and her folks became even more friendly. Then one night her father asked Bud a question.

“What are you plans for after the war, Bud?”

“Hopefully college, for some sort of profession,” Bud said. “I need to make a good living.”

“How about living here, in England,” said her father. “You could be a purser on one of our ships. You know, the chap that handles the money and such.”

“Hadn’t thought about leaving the States,” said Bud. “All my ties are back there.”

“Well, think about it,” said his host, looking slyly over at Nora. “It could work out well, especially if you were a member of our family.”

Bud ignored the hidden suggestion. And it was a good thing he did. The very next day he was ordered to report for full-time duty. The war was heating up again.

Finding just enough time to go see Nora, he told her he was back in the Army completely, and might not see her again.

"Too bad," she said. "I had hoped you would have me pregnant by now, so you would come back to England, as my dad suggested. Besides, my parents want grandchildren as soon as possible. Promise you will come to see me when the war is over."

Bud promised, but he knew he was lying. And he decided to never tell her about his sterility.

CHAPTER SEVEN, The Crusade in Europe

Within a few days Bud's platoon was put on a landing craft, and ferried across the English Channel to France. Their landing area was called Omaha Beach, and there were hundreds of such boats coming ashore in waves. Bud's boat became hung up on some underwater obstructions, so several of his troops started to jump off too soon. His yelling at them that they might drown stopped their exodus. Soon the boat drivers wangled the release of the boat backwards, then came forward between obstacles. Charging ahead on the sand, Bud's group suffered many casualties from a machine gun in a pillbox on the hill above the beach. Knowing something had to be done, Bud grabbed an explosive satchel and ran a zigzag pattern up to the pillbox and threw it through one of the openings. The explosion blew the pillbox to smithereens.

But in running back down the hill, a shell exploded behind him, sending a piece of shrapnel into his left buttocks. A medical corpsman grabbed him and removed the fragment immediately, and bandaged the wound. Bud kept going.

And so it went as they advanced through the countryside, through one town after another—towns whose names he couldn't remember. Bud had no hesitancy about taking chances. His own machine gun operation set an example for the members of his platoon. Liberating one town after another over the next few days, his group was mugged by men and women alike with welcoming hugs and kisses.

Eventually coming to a river, he was informed that only one bridge was left on which to cross it. Spotting a trio of enemy men on the under girding works getting ready to dynamite the bridge, Bud leaped into a boat tied up on shore, rowed out into the river, and cut loose with his gun. The men fell into the river.

"That was reckless," said his company commander, when he came back up on the bridge, "but you might get a medal for it."

"I just didn't want anything to happen to that bridge," said Bud.

When they came into Paris, the welcoming was uproarious. Bud's cohorts could not get enough of the girls grabbing them.

Then the Army settled down to clean up work, until Bud found himself in Belgium in the winter snows. Suddenly the enemy was pushing back, and Bud got shot. He heard much later that it was called the Battle of the Bulge—when the enemy "bulged" through the lines in a last ditch effort. And he would get hurt. The bullet tore through his left shoulder, so he was evacuated from that snowy area and eventually shipped back Stateside.

Settling into the routine of Army hospital life as he healed, Bud became acquainted with many of the employees. One of the nurses introduced herself as Donna. Even in his wounded state, he could appreciate the way she filled out her uniform. She not only seemed to enjoy examining him, but would lean on the foot of his bed with her blouse unbuttoned slightly, revealing round firm appendages to tease him. He did not know anything about her personal life, and was never to learn about it either.

One day he said, "You're slowly killing me."

"Not really," she said. "Just trying to entertain you a little. I notice in my exams of you that they grow 'em big where you come from."

Yep," he said. "I'm six foot two, as is my father."

"That's not what I mean, and you know it," she said, smiling, as she left the ward he was in. "Some day I'm going to sample that."

As Bud healed he got bored, and asked the hospital personnel if there was something he could do to help out. So they put him to work emptying waste baskets. He pushed a four-wheeled cart up and down the aisles, dumping the contents of the waste baskets in a large container on it. Boring work, but better than just lying in a bed all day. One day as he went by a supply room, Donna stepped out and grabbed him, pulling him through the door, and locking it behind them.

"Now!" she whispered, handing him a condom.

"Yep, now!" he said back.

Off came the proper garments, followed by immediate insertion. This, then, became a regular activity. Bud got great satisfaction from her, and he believed she got it from him.

Several months in an Army hospital slowly put Bud back together. All that was left was a large scar, but he felt no lasting pain from the wound. The scar from the slight wound from the shrapnel in his butt was hardly noticeable. Although he was told to report to a veterans' hospital on a regular basis, the Army discharged him, and sent him home. He knew he would miss Donna, and hoped she felt the same about him. He never saw her again.

CHAPTER EIGHT, Back Home

As Bud rode the bus towards Pennington he wondered how many people would be left there who knew about his condition. He had almost decided to keep it as much of a secret as he could. As a means to that end, although he had no real plans to use them, he had acquired a pocket full of condoms. When the Post Exchange had been closed on the Army base where he had received his discharge, they had disposed of all stock—giving it all freely to soldiers passing through. Bud had taken a dozen pairs of khaki shorts and as many undershirts, and he didn't know why at the time, but he had absconded with a roll of about fifty condoms—all linked up in containers like a large segmented worm.

As he got off the bus in town, the first person he saw was Jim, the Jim of the river camping experience. Jim ran over and shook hands, then linked their arms.

"Stash your bag in the bus station and come with me," he said.

"Where are we going?" inquired Bud.

"To sign up for Rockin' Chair money," said Jim. "The government gives us returning servicemen twenty dollars a week for a while to get us adjusted. We pick up forty dollars every two weeks, which is the only time you can sign up. Even then you don't get your first check for a month. And today is the day. If you don't sign up today, you have to wait two more weeks just to sign up, and you won't get any money for six weeks. Sign up today and you'll get it in a month."

"I plan on going to college, as soon as I can get registered," said Bud. "I went through the G.I. Bill instructions when I was discharged. I suppose you did too."

"Yeah, we all had to do that," said Jim.

"What's the job situation like, Jim?" asked Bud. "I don't expect to need one, but just in case."

"There's nothing, Bud," said Jim. "All the 'early outs' got what few coal mine jobs there were—but those are all highly technical now—big equipment, long wall mining, strip mining, no pick and shovel work anymore. I heard the power plant at the Pocket is hiring a lot of men—but it's just for a big expansion program, and they will be let go when it's completed."

"Not much to look forward to, except school, then," said Bud.

"Yep," said Jim, "but this Rockin' Chair is better than nothing. So let's get you registered."

As they walked along, Bud asked, "What's with you and Ruby now?"

"Kind of a tragedy," said Jim. "My plan was to come back from the Navy and spend the rest of my life with her. I do not know what she was doing when working down there at Oak Ridge while I was in the Navy, but I came home to find her infected with syphilis. They had suspended a lot of her operation down there, so she was home. We were intimate the first night I was back, but it was dark. The next day I saw her in the light, and remember all those venereal disease movies and slides they showed us in the service? Well, she showed all the symptoms."

"What did you do?" asked Bud.

"I got us both to the doctor," said Jim. "She had it, but I didn't. Glad I used a rubber on her. I gave her 200 dollars and put her on a bus for Knoxville. I hope the hospital down there is curing her. She never told her parents—just pretended she was going back to Oak Ridge."

Never thought of that, thought Bud. *Could have happened to me in England. Maybe that's another reason to be glad I have the condoms. Well, at least he had a chance at a life with one woman, something I don't have. I'll probably go from one to another all my days.*

Later in the day, Bud was welcomed home by his parents, and he had the opportunity to tell them about his plans for college, and how the G.I. Bill would pay for it. He planned to register for it the following Monday.

On Saturday Bud learned of a tent meeting being held in Woodway. Something different to do, so he decided to go. He had always enjoyed church singing, but not the preaching. He thought that if he sat in the back of the tent, he could sneak out when the preaching started.

As he walked down the road towards the tent, a young girl came rushing out of a house on the way, and proceeded to walk along with him.

"Hi," she said, to which he replied likewise.

She said no more, and neither did Bud. She went in the tent with him, and sat next to him. Getting a better look at her, he saw short dark hair, brown eyes, black patent leather shoes at the ends of long tan legs sticking out from under a short white summer dress.

A pretty picture, he thought.

When he got up to leave the tent, she went with him. On the way back to her home, he learned that her name was Mary Ann, that she was a senior in high school, and that since her father ran a tavern in Norfolk, he had moved his family to Woodway to live with Mary Ann's grandmother until the east coast dangers of the war had passed. Telling her goodnight at her gate, he arranged to take her to a movie in neighboring Big Stone Gap, about thirty miles away, the next day.

When she slid in the front seat of his father's car next to him the next afternoon, the skirt of her short light blue summer dress crept up very high—and she either did not know it, or chose to ignore it. Beyond greeting him, she said very little on the trip to their destination. She kept patting him on the thigh as they drove, which Bud just saw as a friendly gesture—not reading anything into it.

It was dark when they came out of the theater, and Mary Ann slid over close to Bud in the car. Again, with her knees propped up, her skirt was revealing a lot of her legs. As they drove, she took his right hand, and placed it on her bare left thigh. Getting the message, Bud massaged her leg all the way up. Pulling off into an entrance to a farm field, he turned towards her and with her cooperation, removed her panties. She was slightly awkward, but Bud could not even guess if this was her first time or not. Bud was glad he had stuck a couple of rubbers in his pocket. Mary Ann did not need to know about his sterility.

As they drove on down the road, she started massaging him in sensitive places, so he pulled off again the first chance he got. This time she was not nearly as awkward. Later she kissed him goodbye at her gate, still having said very little on the whole time of their date. She had revealed, however, that her catching up with him the night before was her mother's idea, when they saw him coming down the road. She said her mother wanted her to have a boyfriend.

I wonder just how much of a boyfriend she was supposed to have, he thought.

On Monday, Bud caught the bus to Blacksburg, by way of Roanoke—and to disappointment. The registrar at Virginia Polytechnic Institute said he would be glad to accept his registration, but it would be another year before he could start school. He spent the night at the YMCA in Roanoke, then caught the bus to Harrogate, Tennessee, going right on through Pennington. The registration office at Lincoln Memorial University there told him about the same thing VPI did—it would be a while before he could start. He caught the bus home with his tail between his legs.

The next day he was accepted for temporary work at the Pocket power plant. It paid well, even if it would not last long. At least he now had time to figure things out. He arranged for transportation with a neighbor who was already working there, too.

At the end of his first week's work Bud was invited to a house party to celebrate somebody's birthday in Woodway. He did not even know the people having the gathering, but they seemed to be inviting all the young people around there. He did not normally enjoying such affairs, with all the "innocent" kissing games and such, but he was bored. As the party wore on, he found himself sitting on the front porch with a voluptuous young redhead, among other people.

Coming over and sliding in the swing beside him, she whispered, "I'm Anna, Janet's younger sister. You remember her?"

Of course he did.

"She went off to college and got married," said Anna. "Let's go for a walk."

As they went hand-swinging across the moonlit back yard of the house, Anna stopped him with a warm, wet friendly kiss. Then she spread the towel she was carrying on the grass, lay down on it, and pulled him down on top of her.

"Janet told me about you," she said. "Is it true?"

"Do you mean was I good to her?" Bud said. "Of course I was."

"Yes, and really good to her, I bet. Hope you can be just as good to me."

Soon Anna's panties were removed, as well as Bud's trousers, and they were doing what he and Janet had done—only Anna was dynamite by comparison. She couldn't get enough, and neither could he. For Bud there had been a few women, but he couldn't even guess if Anna had done this before or not. It didn't matter to him. He had never lived in a virgin world. After that night, Anna was always ready, almost anywhere, and anytime. This pattern with her was to be repeated many times, probably until his job at the Pocket ran out—if it hadn't been for Rene, and her mother.

One Saturday Bud decided to check out his old stomping grounds around the swirl hole. As he cut across some yards in Woodway to get to the Odd Fellows Tabernacle on foot, he heard somebody call his name. Looking around, he spotted a young girl on a porch of a nearby house.

Walking over closer, he said, "You know my name?"

"Yeah, Jim told me you were home, and explained who you were," she said. "Where are you going down this way?"

"I'm heading on a hike to the swirl hole behind the old tabernacle," he answered. "I used to fish down there. Just looking around and reminiscing."

"Want some company?" she asked. "I'm not doing anything."

When he invited her along, she revealed that her name was Rene, she had just graduated from high school, and that her father had recently lost his life in the war. As she walked along beside him, he noticed that she had a certain bounce in her step that translated all the way to her ample bosom and healthy hips. Her smiling brown eyes glowed her friendship, and her friendly chatter reflected her outgoing personality. She was wearing yellow shorts and top, and sandals—which she kicked off when they arrived at the secluded place on the river. Bud sat down on a grassy patch, leaning sleepily back against a log to reflect on their surroundings. He had always liked this place—and having Rene along today made it even more pleasant.

Later, shouting, "Hey Bud, I'm going swimming," she woke him from the nap he had dozed off into.

Looking up, he saw her laying her clothes on the log, and her nude body entering the river. Motioning him to join her, she swam away underwater. Bud stripped off his clothes and joined her.

"You know how it is with young girls, Bud," she said, giggling. "Look but don't touch. Of course, with old girls, you can touch all you want to, just don't look."

But soon Bud was both looking and touching. He had to admit to himself that she was a fine specimen of womanhood—and he was aroused by just looking. Soon they were entwined on the grass, touching, feeling, enjoying, dreaming.

Bud kept thinking, for the thousandth time, he guessed, *Why can't I have something like this permanently?*

But he knew it would not last. She probably already knew about his sterility, because Jim probably told her—so this was just a fun thing to do temporarily, while waiting for something better to come along for her. Besides she had already told him she was heading off to college come fall.

When they finally arrived back at her house, she introduced him to her mother, Irene—a surprisingly delightful thirty-six year old war widow, with a figure like Rene's. The two women invited him to have supper with them, which he agreed to do. The lively conversation belied the activities of Bud and Rene earlier in the day. Their visit was straight-laced and proper—but overly friendly. Promising to come see them again, Bud hiked on home.

A couple of days later he found himself in that part of Woodway again, so he decided to stop in and see Rene. Her mother was sitting in a chair on the porch, dressed about the way Rene had been the other day. After informing Bud that Rene was not at home right now, she asked him if he would like a glass of iced tea. When he said yes, she went in the house to fix it, while he found a chair on the porch. Soon Irene called him to come in the house. Walking through the living room into the kitchen, he met Irene coming towards him with her top removed, lovely bare breasts protruding.

"I'm getting cool," she said. "Do you like me this way?"

He assured her she looked wonderful. She put her arms around him, snuggling her bare bosom against him. Then she backed away, and removed her shorts and panties.

"Maybe you would like me better like this," she said, smiling.

A few minutes later and they were in her bedroom, with her spread-eagled on the bed.

"It's been a while," she said. "I hope I still remember what to do."

And it was obvious to Bud that she had not forgotten anything. And that was to be the start of another routine. Whenever Rene was home, they found a place to go. Whenever she was not, her mother entertained Bud on her bed, her couch, her living room floor, or anywhere else she deemed a fit place.

Bud hardly ever thought about Mary Ann anymore. She had been kind of a dud anyway. But he was enjoying the best of several worlds. His power plant job was working out well, neither Anna or Rene, both always sure things, although with college plans for the fall, were pressuring him to get married, and Irene was probably secure in enjoying her dead husband's insurance, plus a lifelong war widow's pension. His return to his home had not worked out exactly as he had planned—keeping people in the dark about his condition—but even with these three women knowing his secret, as he presumed they did, it was a good way to live, for now anyway.

CHAPTER NINE, Dayton

When the Pocket power plant positions were eliminated, Bud told his dad he had to do something which might mean moving away—and his parents accepted that. His dad said that he had a cousin in Dayton, Ohio, who might be of help to Bud if he chose to go there—and most of the manufacturers in that city were hiring. So Bud caught the bus to Dayton, with changes in Middlesboro and Cincinnati. His father's cousin told him he could sleep on a bed they had in the basement, if he was not too fussy. Bud welcomed it as a frugal opportunity. A few days later he was hired as an electric motor test technician at Delco on the second shift. Bud had some idea that he might be able to take some classes during the daytime.

At the end of his first day's work, when he came home and collapsed in his bed about midnight, he had a visitor. She was about his age—very tall and very heavy, and said she was his father's cousin's daughter, Amy. She worked days in another plant. Bud was too tired to spend much time with anyone, so she welcomed him and disappeared back upstairs. When Saturday rolled around, and Bud was visiting with his relatives, she came into the living room. She was wearing a black skirt and white blouse, and shoes with medium heels. Light blue eyes, light brown hair, chunky in the torso, big legs, but everything seemed proportioned right for a large girl. Not too bad. She seemed nice enough. Bud enjoyed exchanging pleasantries with her. She asked him if he would like to go to a movie with her, and he said yes. Looking through the daily newspaper at the listings for the dozen or so theaters, they selected one, and when the proper time arrived, set out—catching a streetcar downtown. When they returned home close to midnight, and Bud went to bed, soon Amy came downstairs wearing a thin cotton housecoat, and nothing else. She smiled as she removed it and slid into bed with Bud.

"The folks are asleep," she said. "I'm glad you are not."

Soon they were wrapped in each others arms, and stayed that way most of the night. As the biggest woman he had ever been with, she was most delightful.

"This will be your typical Saturday night from now on," she whispered later. "And maybe some other nights, too."

Well, so much for my lack of recreation, thought Bud.

And she meant it. From then on, as long as he lived at his relatives' house, she made herself available—no matter where he had been, who he had been with, or what he had been doing. She wanted nothing else—just a roll in the hay.

In Bud's job at Delco he and the other electric motor testers did their inspecting on an assembly line in which the units came along on a moving belt. As the motors were approved, the testing personnel took them off the line and placed them on skids. The problem was that there never were enough skids, so someone had to ramble around the floors of the plant pulling a wheeled skid mover searching for them. Bud did not particularly like that duty, but since he was low man on the totem pole, he got stuck with it quite often.

One day when he was extracting a stack of skids from a storage place on another floor, he heard a voice say, "Those are a dollar apiece. You can pay me, and I take only cash."

Looking around he discovered Miss Personality herself—all dishwater blond curls over blue eyes and freckles, smiling beautifully.

Taking the bull by the horns, he pulled out his billfold and said, “What else do I get for my money?”

“I don’t know. What would you like?”

“I’d like for you to go to a movie with me Saturday night! How ‘bout it?”

“Not until we are properly introduced.” She said. Then turning to a co-worker, said, “Louise, introduce me to this character, will you?”

Taking the cue, Louise said, “Character, this is Frances. Frances this is Character.”

“Actually it’s Bud,” he said. “Tell me where to pick you up. I’m too poor to have a car, so we will have to ride a bus or streetcar.”

So Bud and Frances had their first date of many—and for him, an enjoyable one. He learned she had grown up in Maysville, Kentucky, as had many of her co-workers. As time went on, they did many things together—movies, dances, amusement parks, picnics. Bud made no untoward moves towards her, and she did none toward him. Then one evening they returned from a date, and no one was home at the house where she lived. Bud was sitting on the couch, and she sat down on the floor between his legs, with her knees propped up in front of her, asking him to massage her shoulders—which he did. Then he reached down and slid her skirt up to the tops of her hose, which were held up by a garter belt.

“That’s far enough,” she whispered, as she arose and sat beside him on the sofa.

“It’s never far enough,” he whispered back, as he slid his hand up her thigh.

Before long he had removed her panties, with her help.

“That’s cute,” he whispered, running his hand across a large brown birthmark in the silken hair of her crotch, showing now that her panties were gone.

“They run in my family,” she giggled. “My dad has one on his shoulder. But I guess I’m the only one who has one there.”

Soon she was writhing with pleasure as he stroked the birthmark, then went even further. Soon they were locked in a loving embrace—filled with sighs of passion until they were both spent. Afterwards she started to cry.

“Did I hurt you, Frances?” he said, holding her close.

“No, that was marvelous,” she said. “But what if I’m pregnant? How could I face my family?”

“You won’t be,” he said, then he was telling her why not.

She appeared greatly relieved, and stopped crying to laugh.

“Do you want me to leave?” he asked.

“Oh, no. You can’t leave me now. Not ever!”

Over the next few weeks Bud and Frances became intimate many times, and his sterility did not seem to bother her at all. They had gotten so close, he was not being with Amy when he got home evenings, and was seriously considering asking Frances to be his wife. Then on a Monday at Delco he got the shock of his life!

Again he had used his skid search excuse while working to go down to Frances’ floor in the factory to see her. But she was not there. When Louise, the one of her work friends who had given them the fake introduction many weeks ago, spotted him and came over to where he was.

“I’m afraid I have bad news for you Bud,” she said. “Frances went back home to Maysville for the weekend, as we all do sometimes. But she ran into an old boyfriend and they eloped and got married. She had told her mother about you, who told me Frances said she thought you would understand. I don’t know what she meant by that, and I do not know if she is coming back here to work.”

Another opportunity for a stable life shot all to hell, thought Bud, as he glumly hauled his load of skids back up to his work floor.

So he went back to having fun with Amy, his big distant cousin. But the Frances story was not over. Two weeks went by, and Bud found himself back on Frances' work floor. Louise saw him and came over to talk.

"Frances didn't come back?" he asked.

"Yes and no," said Louise. "Her mother said she's back in Dayton, but working somewhere else. Sad story. While on their short honeymoon, her old-boyfriend new-husband confessed to Frances that he married her only to spite some other girl. She left him in tears, and came back to Dayton. She's working in a dress-making shop on a downtown street. She doesn't want to see anyone—won't even accept our calls."

"But I'd like to talk to her," said Bud. "We once had something. Maybe we could again."

"I don't know," said Louise. "She probably feels guilty about what she did to you."

Bud tried calling her, to no avail, so one afternoon he just barged into the dressmaking shop where Louise told him Frances worked. She looked up, saw him, turned red-faced, then dropped her eyes and ran out the back door. Sticking his hands in his pockets, Bud trudged out to the sidewalk and headed for home.

When fall rolled around, Bud registered at the University of Dayton as an Industrial Engineering student, and started classes—scheduling them to meet his work schedule. He really liked the math classes, but didn't care much for one instructor, a Mr. Gebhart—who was older, almost of retirement age, and apparently just didn't feel like working any more.

Bud was sharing classes with a variety of characters, but the one that impressed him most was a no-nonsense veteran of the Air Force—a colonel who had been one of the first P-38 pilots.

He had a skull and crossbones tattooed on his left bicep. One day when Bud got up enough nerve to ask him about it, the Colonel told him he had been a motorcycle racer before the war, and that was when he got the tattoo. After that the Colonel sort of adopted Bud, who was six years his junior.

One day the Colonel asked Bud to encourage as many students as possible to stay after class. Most of them did. Then the Colonel approached Mr. Gebhart.

"Mr. Gebhart," he said. "You are being paid to teach us math, but you are not doing it. You sit up there in a window and watch the football team practice down on the field below. And we are not learning any math. I suggest you start earning your salary."

"I'll flunk you, Sir," Gebhart said, getting red in the face, "and the rest of you, too."

"No, you won't," said the Colonel. "I will report you to the university president, and if that doesn't get results, I'll go to the Veterans' Administration. Over eighty percent of the men students here are vets on the G.I. Bill, and the VA is paying for our education. I'm sure they would like to get their money's worth."

Bud noticed that not only did Gebhart became his best teacher after that, but as time went on, Gebhart and the Colonel became the best of friends.

A fellow but female engineering student named Mary Martha was eleven years older than Bud. She was a former Women's Army Corps member, and had a silver plate in her head from a jeep accident in Europe in WWII. One day she, Bud and the Colonel came out of that math class, and she remarked that there were no students' rest rooms on that fourth floor of St. Joseph's Hall, and it was too far to the closest one. The Colonel marched over to the door that said FACULTY LADIES ROOM on it, and ripped the sign off, throwing it in the nearby waste basket. Some guy in a suit came out of the adjoining men's faculty rest room and berated the Colonel. Bud simply walked over to the men's room, and ripped the sign off it, too. The suit never said a word, beating a hasty retreat to the nearest stairs. Their female cohort was all smiles, as she entered the ladies room. Bud waited for her, and walked her to her car. He met her for lunch on succeeding days, and they became good friends.

He enjoyed her stories, like the one about her religion.

"I'm Catholic, or once was," she told him. "When I enrolled here at this Catholic university, some of the Christian Brothers and a Jesuit priest kept encouraging me to come back to the Church. Finally I decided to, so I went clear out to Drexel, a far western and fairly new suburb to a new church to go to confession—something I had not done for over fifteen years. Nobody would know me out there. As our discussion went on, that priest started in to lecture me. So I told him I had not come out there for a sermon, just for confession, and if he didn't stop I was going to leave. You know what he said? He said, 'And if you do, Mary Martha, I'll come right out and bring you back!' He was one of my instructor priests here at the university, just filling in out there when needed!"

One day when they were discussing personal problems, he told her about his sterility. She just accepted it, and she and Bud started to get it on almost immediately after that day, and they made no bones about it—openly discussed it, as well as the possibility of VD. They both agreed that they were clean from any possibility. Based on her knowledge of sexual positions and activity, Bud suspected she had experienced about as many men as he had women. But as usual, his closeness with Mary Martha was just physical—enjoyable, but just physical, no depth to it.

CHAPTER TEN, Part Time Jobs

Bud wanted to go to school continuously—including summer—but he learned that the classes he wanted to schedule for that period were later in the day, and would interfere with his second shift factory job. The G.I. Bill paid him seventy-five dollars a month subsistence—not enough to live on, even as frugally as he was being—but almost any kind of part time job would suffice. He found one in the concession stand in a drive-in theater, which was advertised on the university bulletin board. The manager told Bud he had decided to recruit college students because the local employees were robbing him blind. The theater was in an unsavory neighborhood anyway, and the help had no qualms about such rackets as giving five dollars in change to their friends when being paid with a one dollar bill. The place was open about nine months of the year, and Bud would be going to work at six in the evening. There were eleven such places around Dayton, all run by the same company.

After a month of serving pop, popcorn, hotdogs and candy, Bud knew the operation very well. That's when the manager quit, because his full time job became too much—so Bud was made manager. He liked the higher salary, but he had to stay late to do inventory and bookwork every night, then go by the bank to make a night deposit of his concession stand's nightly earnings. His two key employees were May, a forty-year-old serious lady, who cooked hotdogs, and her daughter-in-law, Rosie, who popped the popcorn. He had to hire two more college students to help him with the pop, candy, and ice cream.

He became friends with the couple who managed the theater, and appreciated their sense of humor. One night during intermission, the manager announced over the loud speaker that there were two people there who were married to someone else, and that the mate of one of them was at the box office looking for trouble. If the couple would just drive out, no questions would be asked. The theater didn't want any trouble. The ruse was that the manager had arranged for two friends of his to just drive away. Both he and Bud were shocked when three cars left, two with wheels spinning.

Another night, when the manager was not there, his wife mentioned to Bud that two of the "moonlights" at the back of the theater were burned out, and the bulbs needed replacing. These were four colored lights mounted about fifty feet up on metal supports, which flooded the whole theater with modified light—so it would not be so dark. Bud told her he would replace the bulbs—heights had never bothered him. Climbing up the supports by the extensions in place for that purpose, he stepped out on a platform below the lights and replaced the bulbs. When he had gotten back down about halfway, a convertible automobile backed in under him, containing two people. They immediately climbed into the back seat, removed part of their clothing, and started making passionate love—while Bud hung onto his perch, looking straight down on their activity. After they were finished, he slid on down, told them goodnight, and watched them cruise away—wheels throwing gravel.

Several weeks into the summer Bud came out to the old Chrysler Airflow he had been able to purchase to drive to school and to his job, and a young blond woman was sitting in it. Everyone had already gone home, and he had stayed later, as usual, to do his management chores.

"HI, Bud," she said. "I'm Holly. Hope you'll drive me home."

Appalled at her brazenness, he agreed to do so—but told her had to go to the bank first. He thought he had seen her around the drive-in before, but could not be sure. As he drove away, she swiveled around in the seat with her legs propped up towards him, with her thighs exposed out from under her short summer skirt. After he made his night deposit at the bank, she slid over close and started stroking him. Soon they were parked in the rear of the bank's parking lot, rocking the old Chrysler's back seat. On the way to where she directed him to drive her home, he stopped at an all-night gas station. When the attendant was servicing the car, he kept eyeballing first Bud then Holly. When Bud got out to pay him, he saw it—a condom he had used so that this new girl would not know about his condition was stuck just above the gas tank lid. Apparently, when Bud had discarded it out the window, it had stuck on the car. Embarrassing!

The next evening May said to Bud, "Did Holly get you to drive her home last night?"

"Well, yeah," said Bud, quizzically. "She was in my car when I finished up."

"She's a little wild, Bud, a little boy crazy. She's my daughter, you know," said May. "I don't know what I'm going to do with her. Be careful around her. She just turned fifteen."

Bud just stood looking at May, slack-jawed. Of course he was never with Holly again.

After the Holly episode, Bud fairly well planned to avoid women as much as possible. So far none of the many girls he had known intimately had gotten him into trouble, but some could—especially one as young as Holly. He decided to concentrate on his education and career. He found a small apartment which he could afford, and moved away from Amy.

The couple, Paul and Marie, who owned it, had remodeled their house so they could live downstairs and have two small apartments upstairs. It was near a streetcar line, which he liked, in case he did not want to drive somewhere, since parking was a problem. He learned the other tenant was a young woman—a niece of the owners with a toddler daughter. Marie babysat her, along with their own little girl, while her mother worked. Paul was in the tree service business, and worked a lot of hours—especially after a thunderstorm would damage many trees.

After a few days of living there, Bud met his neighbor. One Sunday afternoon she knocked on his door.

"Hi, I'm Betty, your neighbor," she said. "Want to come over for a cup of coffee? My daughter is taking a nap."

So Bud joined her that day, and several other days. They became good friends. Bud thought she was attractive—always well-dressed, for her job, probably. Eventually it came out, from Marie to Bud, that Betty was not married, that she had gotten pregnant by her soldier boyfriend—and was thrown out of her home by her horrified parents, and taken in by Paul and Marie. Then her boyfriend was killed before they could get married. Betty hated her folks.

"Could have happened to anybody," said Marie, with great understanding.

When the theater closed for the winter, Bud found lucrative, by comparison, employment at Midwest, a tool and die shop, in their design department, where he could put his math and drafting ability to good use. In a few months the shop began to run out of work, and started to lay people off. Bud knew that was the nature of that type of subcontracting work, but he thought he had lucked out. On a Monday the chief design engineer came back to Bud's drawing board to tell him that his job was secure, since he was doing design work for National Cash Register, and NCR paid Midwest to keep one designer for them. But then on Friday, the chief let him go—no work for NCR was available.

Bud went home feeling pretty sad, and moped around home for the evening—until Betty came over for a visit.

"I know something's eating you, Bud," she said. "Care to tell me about it?"

By the time he finished telling her about his job situation, she had her arms around him, holding him tightly.

"I'd like to do more to please you, if you want me to," she said. "But my last romance ended in a tragedy. I do not want anything like that again."

Bud kissed her hungrily, then told her why she had nothing to worry about. They spent the night in the warmth of each others arms.

But Bud was to learn that job-shop people stick together. His ex-boss called around to the other job shops and found a position for Bud. He could start Monday.

International Tool was the biggest job shop in Dayton and seemed to always be busy. They had what looked to Bud like a permanent help wanted sign on the front of the building. So between quarters of school he decided to apply for a design job there. Stopping in before going to work one morning, he obtained an application, which was a five by eight inch card, from the girl at the front desk, and hurriedly filled it out. She made a phone call, and soon a tall, thin white–haired man got out of the nearby elevator. She handed him the application.

He scanned it briefly, then turned to Bud, saying, "Boy, you are going to have to learn to letter better than this in order to work here."

Then he tore up the application, threw it in the wastebasket close by, and got back in the elevator.

Bud was much chagrinned. Lettering was his one design trait of which he was most proud. He knew he was better than any designer he had ever worked with. That morning he was just in a hurry to get to his job. He stewed about it for a week. On Monday he decided to try it again.

I'll show him, he thought.

This time he filled the application with his best printing. Same scenario—the white-haired guy scanned his card.

Then he said, "When you come to work here tomorrow, take this elevator to the third floor, sit on a chair outside my office until I come out to tell you what to do. Your hourly pay is two dollars and thirty cents."

Bud was high as a kite. The pay was a dollar an hour more than he was getting! He had no qualms about quitting his present job with no notice. If they had laid him off it would have been that way.

Bud's increased income came at a good time. Later when he had to quit, in order to finish school, International put him to work part time. The organization had plenty of auto company work at the time, so were working a lot of overtime.

CHAPTER ELEVEN, Old and New Relationships

Then Bud got a letter from Nora, back in England. She told him she was flying to Canada to visit an uncle, and wanted to come on down to Dayton to visit Bud. He had mixed emotions about it, but agreed that she should come, and wrote to tell her so. He met her at the airport, and their hugs and kisses were warm. They were glad to see each other. Their night in the Biltmore in each others arms was warm and satisfying—as were the next few nights. No mention was made of him moving to England.

On the last day of her visit, she said, "I learned of your job at the dairy farm before joining the shipyard. So I went out there for a visit. I didn't meet Cornelia. One of her assistants told me her Navy boyfriend got killed in the south Pacific, and she was still shook up about it."

"That's too bad," said Bud, sorrowfully. "She seemed very devoted to him."

Bud wisely never mentioned his intimacy with Cornelia. Maybe Nora had already guessed what it was.

"I'm getting married, Bud," she said. "Of course if you got me pregnant this past week, like I wanted you to in England, I don't know how my guy might react."

Then Bud told her about his sterility.

"How come you didn't tell me before?" she asked. "I don't think it would have bothered me. Might have bothered my parents, but not me. I just wanted to be with you."

"I didn't want to destroy what we had," said Bud. "I thought it might drive you away."

"You could still come back to England with me," she said. "I still think we belong together."

"There are two things wrong with that premise, Nora," Bud said. "One is that eventually you would want a family."

"We could probably adopt, if I do," she said. "What is the other problem?"

"This is my home. I couldn't imagine living anywhere else, except in the good old U.S. of A."

'I'm sorry, Bud," she said. "Maybe we just aren't meant to be together."

Later that day, Bud and Nora said their goodbyes for the last time.

It was a warm summer day when Bud and his co-worker, Wally, decided to go for a swim to cool off. The man-made beach was sand hauled in to line the shore of a former gravel pit that was filled by an underground spring. As the two men were diving off the large float out in the lake, Bud spotted a familiar sight coming in the gate—Mary Martha and the Colonel, arm in arm. He swam over to where they were putting their blanket on the sand.

After the greeting hugs and handshakes, Mary Martha said, "As you have probably figured out, we are now a couple. Planning on marriage."

"For some reason, I'm not surprised," said Bud. "I wish you both many years of happiness."

"We are too old to have a family," said the Colonel, "but we need each other."

Then as Bud conversed with them, he got another surprise, coming through the gate was Frances, and she was with a handsome guy. So she had recovered from her failed marriage after all, and could be with another man—just not Bud. Probably wanted a family, too. He remembered much of their intimacy, as he admired how great she looked in a two-piece swim suit.

"See that gal that just came in?" Bud said to his Wally later. "She was once my girlfriend."

"Well, it looks like she has somebody else now," said Wally.

Bud sat real still for a while, watching Frances and her boyfriend hug and touch each other on their blanket on the sand.

Then he said, “You know, she has a large birthmark right in her pussy hair. I’m gonna go over and asked that guy if he knows about it.”

As his friend gathered up his stuff and headed for the gate, Bud asked, “Where you goin’?”

“Home,” said Wally. “If you are goin’ to get the shit beat outta you, I don’t want to see it.”

So Bud had second thoughts, and just waved at a startled Frances as he left. She was just part of his past now.

On their way home, his friend asked Bud, “Are you aware of the Box 21 Club?”

When Bud answered that he had heard of it, but did not know what it was, his friend told him it was a volunteer rescue group that helped people in trouble, like in fires or floods or snow and ice storms.

“We have all our own equipment, such as boats and four-wheel drive pickup trucks,” said Wally. “You ought to join.”

So a few days later Bud was being indoctrinated into the Box 21 Club.

Their first rescue was at El Dorado Flats, a batch of nondescript houses and house trailers located on the Miami River upstream from Dayton, which flooded every time it rained heavily. The Box 21 members slid their boats off trailers into the river and hauled the residents out to safety. Bud couldn’t understand why anyone would want to live in such an area in the first place. But he guessed it was cheap.

Then Bud met Wally’s wife, Elsie. After one of their missions, he was invited home with Wally for supper. Elsie was a cute chubby natural blond and mother of their three children. The kids seemed happy to play with Bud, and noisily crawled all over him. Elsie greeted him with an unusually warm hug. Their supper was full of obvious caring for each other, and friendliness on the part of everyone. Bud was delighted with this family.

Then Wally and Elsie invited Bud to attend a celebration with them. Wally's parents were the head officers of the Salvation Army in Dayton, with the rank of Major. Each year the organization held a "Chatauqua" at a church camp on an island in the river downstream from Dayton. It was a week-long session of singing, lecturing, training, eating, and visiting. Bud was having a great time on several visits. On one visit he was asked to pick up Elsie at their home and take her to Chatauqua, since Wally and their kids were already at the gathering.

As they drove along, Elsie said, "Wally told me about your situation. Did he tell you about his?"

"Well no," said Bud. "I presume you mean my sterility. What is Wally's situation?"

"Impotence," said Elsie. "His war wound not only kept him in the hospital for a long time, but left him incapacitated."

"Oh, I'm sorry," said Bud, "especially for you. How has that affected you? Apparently you had three nice kids before it happened."

"Yes, and I do not want any more children," said Elsie. "And Wally is loving to me, even though we cannot climax any touchy-feely togetherness. But I miss it, and sometimes I feel almost desperate to have sex again."

"I guess I can understand that," said Bud. "I miss having a family of my own, sometimes. That's why I enjoy your kids so much."

"Perhaps we can help each other," she said, sliding closer to Bud in the car. "You can not only play with my kids, but you could play with me occasionally too."

"No, I couldn't do that to Wally," said Bud. "I'll admit I've been intimate with other girls, but none were married. I'm not a prude, or anything. I just do not think that would be right."

"Well, if you ever change your mind, let me know," Elsie said. "I've never done anything like that either. But I could, and especially with someone I care about as much as I have grown to care for you."

CHAPTER TWELVE, Personal Situations

As time went on, Bud had little time to think about Elsie's proposition, or any other girls for that matter. His new employer started an expansion program of adding new manufacturing facilities all over the country, and he found himself up to his eyeballs in those projects. It started when the Company hired a consultant to evaluate an existing building for them in another town. Bud found himself in that town for some other reason, so he decided to check out the building. When he appeared at the home company later, he inquired of his boss about what the consultant had recommended.

Upon being told that the professional had recommended that the Company obtain the facility for their own use, Bud said, "That building was used by a small electronics appliance manufacturer, and has a sixteen-foot ceiling all the way through it. But the smallest machine which we would put in there is over twenty feet tall."

"Apparently the consultant did not look up," said his boss, with much chagrin. "He went into great detail about how what we want to do there would fit in perfectly."

A few days later Bud was assigned to the task force planning new facilities, a job which he found not only interesting, but exciting. It meant much travel for years to come, but he had no particular ties to Dayton anyway.

Then they sent him to Tampa, Florida, to plan a facility from scratch. Later they wanted him to stay there and manage the plant. Bud readily fell into the Florida lifestyle—going deep-sea fishing with new friends who had boats, and trying his hand at wild boar hunting in north Florida with a group of outdoorsmen. After buying a house, he even put a pigeon cote on the garage, and got into racing the birds as a hobby.

Several years went by, then he got a call from Wally's father.

"Wally is dead," said the man. "He had bought a motorcycle some months back, and wrecked it last night. He died instantly. We would like for you to be a pall bearer."

So soon Bud was back in Dayton, hugging Elsie and her family, while expressing his sympathy. On subsequent trips to the Company's home plant there, he always made it a point to visit Elsie and her children. Over time it became dinners out for just Bud and Elsie, then within a few months, it turned into him enjoying Elsie's pudgy blond beauty in his hotel bed.

I remember this is what she once wanted, he thought, during their first explosive union.

Obviously Elsie was enjoying their trysts just as much as Bud was, since neither had done anything like this for a long time. Bud began to think seriously about their relationship. He could not make children, and she already had three, with no desires for any more. One evening, after several months of steady lovemaking episodes, he ventured a proposal.

"You know, Elsie, if we were married, this would be a lot easier," he said. "Of course, I would have to get a larger house."

"The Company would have to find a position here in Dayton for you," she said. "I'm sure they could."

"What do you mean?" he asked. "My job is in Florida, and I like it that way."

"Then just forget it," she said. "I would never live down there. We can just go on like we are."

But over the next few weeks Bud knew they couldn't. Apparently Elsie did not care as much for him as she had indicated.

Then Bud's father called him.

"Better come home, Bud," he said. "Both your grandparents are dead. Kind of a freakish situation. Your grandma died of natural causes, then when your grandpa was driving to the funeral home, he ran off the road, rolling his car down a hillside, killing himself. So now we have two funerals simultaneously."

So Bud loaded up his car and started the drive to Jonesville.

Might be nice to see the old area again, he thought, *the countryside, the farm, the Crossroads Store. The Store! Such a happy place! I haven't thought much about it for years.*

Now he found himself looking forward to the trip, even if it was for a sad purpose. But then again, his grandparents were in their eighties—had led full happy lives together.

When Bud walked into the visitation area at the funeral home, the first person he saw was Carmen. And she was beautiful! Even though her magnetic brown eyes were beguiling him from a sad face, they were still her eyes—just as he remembered them. Her trim figure, with enticing hips, butt and bust line, was ensconced in a form-fitting black dress with a rear slit, most appropriate for the occasion. She hugged him tightly, kissing him full on the lips.

"I still love you," she whispered. "I want to talk to you after this is over."

"And I still love you," he said. "I had forgotten how much, until just this minute."

But by the time all the details of the burials were completed and carried out, and Bud was ready to say his goodbyes and head back to Florida. Carmen was nowhere in sight.

I wonder what she wanted to talk to me about, he thought, as he loaded up his car for the trip. *Oh well, she can call me. She knows where I am, or my Dad does, anyway.*

But a couple of weeks later Bud received another call from his dad.

"The lawyers have finished reading the will of your grandparents," he said. "They left the farm and everything on it to you. They had a hired man, who lives just down the road, that did everything for them in more recent years. If you do not want to sell it, you might consider doing that, too. He seems to be doing a good job."

"Maybe I'll come up there and see just what I've got," said Bud. "As soon as I can get a little vacation time."

When he arrived at the farm a few weeks later, he noticed that all the buildings seemed to be in good condition. Apparently the hired man looked after things quite well. Then Bud thought it might be interesting to visit the Crossroads Store. So he hiked off down the unchanged sandy road as he had done so many times before. Sitting on the porch of the store in a wicker chair, reading a book, was a familiar figure in a short summer dress. The garment was held up by thin spaghetti straps over very pretty shoulders. He was thrilled when those bright brown eyes leaped to meet his, followed by her rising quickly to give him an extremely tight hug with kisses on the lips. Carmen was just as glad to see him as he was to see her.

"Okay now, bring me up to date," Bud said to her. "Where have you been, and what have you been doing all these years?"

"Mostly dreaming about you!" she said, eyes flashing. "Couldn't you feel it?"

"No, really," he said. "Have you lived here all this time?"

"Pretty much recently," she said. "But after college at Radford State, I taught at various schools around this part of the state. Then when my parents wanted to give up the store, I came back and took it over. I teach at the Jonesville school, and run the store with part-time help."

"I'm sorry we could not see more of each other when my grandparents died, but it was a hectic time."

"Yes, I wanted to tell you something, then," she said.

"Are you married? Do you have a family?"

"No, I would never be happy married to anyone except you, Bud. You have always known that."

"I guess so, and you know the reason we could not do that."

"I know your reasoning for it, but I never bought it," she said, "and that's why I wanted to talk to you. Would you marry me today if that reasoning was not there? How's that for a proposal?"

"You know I would! I've always loved you," said Bud. "But I still cannot make babies."

"Well, that reason is gone," Carmen said. "Sometime back I had some female trouble—some sort of infection. Maybe cancer. They did a hysterectomy on me—you know, where they take away the baby carriage but leave the playpen."

"I'm sorry," said Bud. "Are you alright now?"

"Yes, I'm perfectly healthy," she said. "Perhaps I was getting a little too old to be having babies, anyway, even if I could. But now I'm yours again, if you want me."

"Oh I do, I do!" cried Bud. "I just inherited a farm. Might work out very well for us."

"Jonesville needs teachers for this fall," said Carmen. "Perhaps you could fit in there."

So that's why a few weeks later the man and woman from the farm and the Crossroads Store, as a newly married couple, were driving into Jonesville for their first day of teaching.

As Bud ran his hand up her thigh, which was exposed out from under a short summer skirt, she said, "You better stop that!"

"How long do I have?" he asked.

"Oh, about ten years—maybe twenty," she whispered, as she slid closer in the car, laying her head on his shoulder.

THE END

www.ingramcontent.com/pod-product-compliance
Ingram Content Group UK Ltd.
Pitfield, Milton Keynes, MK11 3LW, UK
UKHW041929190726
13854UKWH00004B/1523

9 781329 576193